Other Avon Flare Books by
Jeanne Betancourt

AM I NORMAL?
DEAR DIARY

JEANNE BETANCOURT writes novels, non-fiction books, screenplays and articles. Her book, SMILE! HOW TO COPE WITH BRACES (Knopf) was named an Outstanding Science Book for Children for 1982. Other books include DEAR DIARY and AM I NOR-MAL? (Avon/Flare) which she also illustrated.

Her upcoming books for kids include a guide for watching television and a young adult mystery romance.

JEANNE BETANCOURT lives in New York City with her husband, her teenage daughter, a cat and a dog named Mop.

Jeanne Betancourt

THE RAINBOW KID

AN AVON CAMELOT BOOK

3rd grade reading level has been determined by using the Fry Readability Scale.

THE RAINBOW KID is an original publication of Avon Books. This work has never before appeared in book form.

AVON BOOKS
A division of
The Hearst Corporation
1790 Broadway
New York, New York 10019

Library of Congress Cataloging in Publication Data

Betancourt, Jeanne.
  The rainbow kid.

  (An Avon/Camelot book)
  Summary: When ten-year-old Aviva comes home from camp to find her parents have separated, she is afraid that instead of being a two-family child, she'll be a two-bedroom, no-family child.
  [1. Divorce—Fiction] I. Title.
PZ7.B46626Rai 1983   [Fic]   83-9979
ISBN 0-380-84665-9 (pbk.)

First Camelot Printing, September, 1983

CAMELOT TRADEMARK REG. U. S. PAT. OFF. AND IN OTHER COUNTRIES, MARCA REGISTRADA, HECHO EN U. S. A.

Printed in the U. S. A.

DON 10 9 8 7 6 5 4 3 2 1

For
Lee Minoff
and for Nicole,
the original Rainbow Kid

CHAPTER ONE

I'M A JOINT CUSTODY KID. MY PARENTS GOT SEPARATED while I was at sleep-away camp last month.

Joint custody means they're going to share me equally. I'll live one week with my mother and one week with my father. I'll keep going back and forth, back and forth.

Mom says I'll be a two-family child.

I say I'll be a no-family child.

I'll have one mother—half the time.

I'll have one father—half the time.

And *no* family.

The only thing I'll have two of is bedrooms.

Aviva Granger, the no-family, two-bedroom child.

Mom got to stay in our old house at 110 Elm Street. It's 106 years old and very cozy.

Dad called this morning to say he finally found a place to live and he wanted me to see it right away. It's over on the other side of town, near the shopping mall.

"You're going to love it, Aviva!" Dad told me as we pushed through the swinging chrome-and-glass doors of the fifteen-story building. "It's fun to live in an elevator building."

Let's just get this over with, I thought as I looked around the lobby—puke green walls, maroon plastic-covered couches, and fake trees. It looked more like a hospital lobby than a place to call home—which is just about right, since this whole divorce business is pretty sick.

My dog, Mop, didn't like the building either—or the divorce business. Sheepdogs are friendly and smart, but walking through the lobby Mop looked mostly confused. He sniffed at a fake tree and gave me his "what-is-the-world-coming-to" look.

Dad's apartment has three rooms: a combination living room/dining room/kitchen all in one normal-size room, and two small bedrooms. I took a deep breath. The apartment smelled brand new and painty, like Merelis's Hardware Store. No one had ever lived there. It was an empty, lonely place.

But Dad was cheery as could be. I guess he was sick of sleeping on his friend Steve's couch.

"And here's your bedroom." He threw open the door with a "Tah-tah!" My room was tiny and white, with only one narrow window looking out on the brick wall of another new building.

Mop poked around looking for a snuggly place to curl up in. There wasn't any.

"So what do you think?" my dad asked me.

I tried to smile. "It's real . . . cute, Dad."

"Well, we need furniture and stuff. There's a sale on beds at Merrick's. You can pick out your new bed. Then we'll go over to Steve's. He's got a couple of old bureaus we can have. This place'll be homey in no time."

I wasn't about to encourage Dad in fixing up his new place. I figured after a few weeks here—especially without a lot of furniture—he might be glad to move back in with Mom and me.

"I can't," I said. "I have to get ready for the first day of school tomorrow. Remember?"

He drove me back to 110 Elm Street but wouldn't come in. Since the separation Dad and Mom act like he never lived there. "I'll bring you back to your mother's," he'll say. And he stops out front without even turning off the motor. He never, ever comes in or sees my mother. They talk on the phone—mostly about me and money.

The rest of the day Mom and I shopped for my school things. I got a denim blue three-ring notebook with a dungaree back pocket on it, a black metal lunch pail like the construction workers use, two new pair of jeans, three T-shirts, and red sneakers.

After supper I put the papers and dividers in my new notebook and colored tiny rainbows in the right-hand corners of the papers.

I loved rainbows way before everybody else. The rainbow became my symbol in kindergarten. Mrs. Mahoney showed us a rainbow out the school window. It was the very first real one I ever saw. Then she taught us how to paint our own rainbows by mixing the three primary colors—red, yellow, and blue. We mixed red and yellow to get orange, yellow and blue to get green, and blue and red to get purple.

When I was in the second grade I painted a rainbow on the wall behind my bed. And last year Mom sewed a big rainbow decal on the back of my dungaree jacket. All my rainbows are the true rainbow colors—the top band is red going to orange to yellow to green to blue, and then to purple on the bottom band.

I hate it when you see faded rainbows with the wrong colors advertising some dumb product like floor wax. Or a grungy bar called The Rainbow Bar and Grill. Cripes.

To me the rainbow stands for love and happiness.

When I finished the thirty-seventh rainbow corner I decided maybe rainbows weren't such a good symbol for me now that our family was divorcing. I just sat there digging my toes deeper and deeper into Mop's furry back and thinking about that.

Mom came into the kitchen and kissed the top of my head. "I have something for you. Now that Dad's got an apartment, he and I figured out when you will be at each house. I made you a calendar to help you keep your schedule straight."

She took a brand-new calendar out of the kitchen drawer. It was the *Movie Monster Calendar* I had wanted for Christmas and didn't get because Mom said it was silly to pay for calendars when the bank and dry cleaner give them to us for free.

She sat down, dug her toes into Mop's back next to mine, and put the calendar in front of us on the table. I didn't say, "Oh, thank you, Mommy!" or "Just what I always wanted," the way she expected. I didn't say anything.

She opened the calendar to September. King Kong was about to drop Fay Wray on MOM written across some weeks and DAD written across others.

"It's mostly regular," Mom said. "One week here, one week there."

The phone rang.

As she ran to answer it I settled back to listen. I might be a detective when I grow up, and telephone conversations are a terrific way to get information. I flipped through the calendar, pretending I wasn't listening.

"Oh, Roy." That was easy. It was my dad.

Detectives look for other clues besides what a person says. Mom hopped up on the kitchen stool and sat on it like it was a horse. She thinks she's pretty modern—wearing jeans and T-shirts and zipping around being a working mother. I watched her. She was fidgeting with the telephone cord, twisting her fingers through the curls. Her voice got louder and edgy. "I thought you were going to come and get all this stuff when we were out."

I could see the pile of things in the hall that Dad was supposed to pick up now that he had an apartment. His old blue duffel bag looked sad slumped against cartons of books.

"Listen," my mom continued. "Don't come up here any later than eleven. This could have been avoided." She hung up with a bang.

My parents are always arguing, more now than before they got divorced. I think they're immature.

Mom tried to put a smile over her grumpy feeling when she came back to the table. She was leaning over my shoulder when I flipped back to Frankenstein's October. I was feeling grouchy and sad myself looking at bunches of MOM days and DAD days. All I wanted were FAMILY days.

"What about my birthday?" I pointed to the unmarked October 31.

Mom sighed. "I don't know yet, but we'll figure it out. All you have to worry about right now is the first day of school. Hurry up. It's already nine o'clock."

I couldn't fall asleep. What would my birthday party be like now that I lived in two places? I kept thinking about the divorce and the beginning of school. I didn't want anyone at school to know (and after all, they might get together again real soon).

After lying there for about twenty thousand hours I tried putting my body to sleep bit by bit.

I whispered to myself, "Your toes are very, very tired. Your toes are falling asleep. Your heels are very, very tired. Your heels are falling asleep. . . ."

The doorbell rang. I heard my dad's voice in the front hall. Then my mom and dad arguing. I tried not to listen and concentrated on putting myself to sleep. "Your stomach is very, very tired. Your stomach is going to sleep."

I got all the way up to my left ear before the floating-sinking feeling of falling asleep finally came.

I'm floating in slow motion over a classroom full of kids. My joint custody calendar with MOM and DAD weeks is all over the blackboards. My mom and dad are arguing in front of the whole class, and all the kids are pointing up at me and laughing.

The next morning my dad's boxes and duffel bag were gone.

CHAPTER TWO

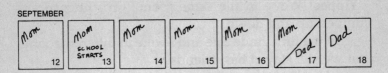

SEPTEMBER

OUR HOUSE IS EXACTLY ONE MILE FROM SAINT AGNES GRAMMAR School, which means it takes me twenty minutes to walk there or ten minutes on the bus. But the first day of school it was raining, so Mom drove me before she went to work. I wanted to get there early to see who was in my class this year. I looked at the postcard from St. Agnes's one more time as we pulled up to the curb. "Report to GRADE SIX, ROOM 410B at 8:30 A.M. on September 13."

St. Agnes School is a big old building with wood floors and high ceilings. The buffed wood floors were already splotched with wet footprints. Poor Mr. Germain. He leaned on his wipe-up mop, pushed back his baseball cap, and shook his head. "Saints have mercy, why does it always have to rain on the first day of school?"

I was so nervous and excited that by the time I got to the fourth floor, elephants were marching in my stomach.

The first kids I saw in 410B were Rita, Janet, and Louise. They stood in a clump at the front of the room so everyone would see them first thing. They're the glamour-girl clique. This is how they talk: "Where did you get that *great* haircut?" Or, "I just *love* your jeans!"

Rita checked me over from head to toe before saying, "Oh, hi, Aviva. What a *terrific* tan. I'm *so* jealous."

Then I saw Sue! Sue's the greatest. She's short, with curly black hair, is full, full, full of life, and is my very best friend. I hadn't seen her all summer.

"Aviva!" She jumped over a chair to get to me. "Yippee! We're in the same room." We hugged and jumped up and down.

In the fifth grade Sue and I were in different rooms, but we still stayed best friends.

"Hey, let's try to sit next to each other," she said. I looked around the room. It was hopeless. Sue was still the shortest girl in the class, and I was still the tallest. Sue always ends up in the first row right under the teacher's nose, and I end up in the back of the room with the big tough guys, like Josh Greene my archenemy.

At that very moment Josh walked into room 410B with the other two worst boys in the sixth grade—Jimmy Johnson and Tommy Cioffi. Josh had on the same gray T-shirt he wore all last year. "Property of Sing Sing Prison," it read on the back.

"Oh, no," I groaned to Sue. "All three of them in one room!" It was going to be awful. Last year just two of those guys drove Mr. Campbell crazy. One day they even threw chalk at him.

Josh Greene mostly drove me crazy. He would whisper his stupid rhymes and copy off my papers. Once I put all the wrong answers on a math test on purpose. If the answer was 2,898, I'd write 2,897. I did the whole paper like that. Then at the last minute, when the papers were being collected, I changed the answers by adding 1 to the last digit. I got a B on that test—ten points off for neatness—but Josh got the F he deserved.

I hate him. A classroom with Josh Greene in it needs an exterminator.

Josh came in yelling "Greene's here. Where's the beer?" He stomped on three chairs and desks with his

14

muddy sneakers to get to the back of the room. Of course his two buddies followed him.

Everybody but me laughed. There wasn't going to be anything funny about this year.

The noise in the room suddenly stopped when a cartful of books came wheeling into the room followed by a clicking of rosary beads, a flutter of black robes, and our first look at our sixth-grade teacher. Five years in a Catholic school and I finally had a nun! All my other teachers were lay teachers—like Mr. Campbell. I'd always wanted a nun. And our nuns are *real* nuns—the old-fashioned kind with white starched linen around their faces and long black robes.

"Oh, boy," Sue gasped. "My brother had her. He said she's tough."

Sister looked us over before she said, "Good morning, class. I'm Sister Bernard Marie. You'll see that there are name cards taped to the corners of the desks. Find yours and take a seat. Quickly now. We have lots to do." She clapped her hands three times, real loud.

Before Sue headed for the front of the room she whispered, "I forgot to tell you; my mom's going to have a baby. Pray it's a girl."

A baby. Two brothers. A mom and a dad. All living together. What a family!

Well, I wasn't going to tell Sue, or anybody else, about my parents' divorce or the joint custody business.

I found my seat—last row, between Josh Greene and Tommy Cioffi. Josh held his nose when I sat down, and Tommy pretended he had to throw up. Sister Bernard Marie didn't even notice.

She was an okay teacher. She gave ordinary homework like math problems and a special long-term assignment to make a "Who Am I?" collage that would show our life in pictures and symbols. You could tell she'd been teaching a long time and wouldn't put up with a lot of nonsense like Mr. Campbell. The three brat-rats didn't show their true colors the first day. I figured they needed time to warm up and plot their war strategy. Sister Bernard Marie better start saying her prayers.

At two-thirty she clapped her hands three times. "All right, everyone. We have just enough time for one more assignment. Put your heading on a clean piece of paper. Then write down the first ten words that come to mind when you think of your summer vacation."

Summer . . . summer. I opened my notebook to page four. I wrote my name and class next to the rainbow. Then, near the margin, I wrote "CAMP." I thought, but didn't write, *divorce, lonely, scared, family dead*. I drew clouds all over my rainbow and made big black raindrops under it.

Camp. I shouldn't have gone. It was a mistake to leave my parents alone. They needed me. A family is just not a family without a kid.

Well, it wasn't too late. Lots of people have separations and get back together, like when Sue and I had a terrible fight in the fourth grade. People just need a little help to straighten things out. And I intended to help my parents. Maybe we would be a family again by my birthday.

I jumped out of my thoughts at the sound of Sister Bernard Marie's voice. "Let me see what you've written, Aviva." She looked at my page with nothing on it but clouds, a dripping rainbow, and the word "CAMP."

Wouldn't you know? Trouble on the first day of school. But Sister just patted me on the shoulder, smiled, and said, "Let's see if this fall can be better than your summer was."

Fat chance, I thought. Josh hit me on the arm the minute Sister's back was turned.

The bell rang. Everyone slammed their books shut and jumped up to leave. Josh and Cioffi were halfway to the front of the room.

Three loud claps. We froze. "I didn't say you could leave. Is the bell the teacher, or is Sister Bernard Marie?"

Dead silence.

"Rather have a bell than an old nun," Tommy Cioffi muttered. Nobody moved. You couldn't be sure by Sister's expression if she heard him or not. Then she said, "Mr. Cioffi stay. Class dismissed."

"I didn't do nothin'," Cioffi protested.

"Well, you're going to do something now," we could hear her saying as we filed out of the room. "Start by washing the boards."

I caught up with Sue in the schoolyard. "What a jerk Cioffi is," I told her.

"You're the jerk, turkey." It was Josh. He grabbed my lunch pail and threw it across the yard. Then he yelled one of his dumb rhymes. "Aviva is the biggest fool in this or any other school." I started to chase him.

I might have caught him, too, if I hadn't bumped into my dad. Dad said he came to meet me to celebrate the first day of school by going out for ice cream. I thought he was just lonely in his silly apartment. At least I hoped so.

I told him all about Sister Bernard Marie and my rotten luck in sitting next to Josh. But Dad was more interested in telling me how he was fixing up the apartment. I didn't pay any attention.

When he was driving me back to Mom's I was thinking, Maybe he'll come in and have supper with us. As we turned into the driveway Mom came rushing out of the house, which is weird because she works until five and it was only about four-thirty. That's when I remembered, I'm supposed to call Mom at her office the minute I get home from school.

She was upset and angry, but she wasn't as mad at me as she was at my dad. "Why didn't you tell me you were picking her up?" she yelled. "It's four-thirty. I was frantic. I left work. I went to the school. I tried to call you."

Mop started barking like crazy at the kitchen door. Mom turned to me. "Aviva, go in and take care of your dog."

I explained, "But it's my fault that—"

"Now!"

I could hear them fighting all the way into my bedroom. Mop kept barking and jumping all over me. I calmed him down by braiding the hair around his ears and thought things over.

I should have asked Dad whether he'd told Mom that he was picking me up. If Mom had known that I was with Dad, then everyone would have been happy and Dad might have stayed for dinner. I started thinking of all the other things I could have done that might have made a difference—like not going to camp in August.

I cut off the little rainbows from the pages of my notebook and threw them in the toilet. They swam around—little rainbow fish—then I flushed them down the toilet. I watched them swirl around and disappear

18

and chanted, "Go, rainbows, go. Down to the sewer, go."

At dinner Mom seemed to have forgotten the fight with Dad. She even made one of my favorite meals—fried chicken and frozen french fries. She wanted to know all about my first day of school.

"I need some family pictures for my collage," I told her.

"What collage?"

"I have to do a 'Who Am I?' collage. We're supposed to collect pictures and things that show who we are. Sister Bernard Marie said to put symbols of ourselves and our families in a box. Next month we'll arrange them on cardboard and show them to the class."

Mom loves it when I have arty kinds of homework. "What a great assignment! Come on." She jumped up and pulled me by the hand. "We'll get that box of old pictures out of my closet."

She took a shoe box of pictures down from a shelf. We sat on the bed and started looking at all these old photos. They weren't in any special order, so first you'd see a picture of me seven years old and then one of Mom pregnant with me.

The ones I like best are those of us on a camping trip in Canada when I was nine. I studied a picture of Mom, Dad, Mop, and me in front of our orange tent. "I guess I can't use this picture," I told my mom. "We're not a family anymore."

"Sure you can." Mom looked a little sad. "We were together then, and we had a lovely time. Use it."

I looked for another family picture. I figured if I could get her to feel sad enough, she might try to figure a way to work things out with Dad.

The phone rang. Mom went around the bed to answer it. Maybe it would be my dad calling to apologize for the fight. That would be perfect, now that she was all sentimental from looking at the camping pictures. I pretended to be looking through the photos while I listened.

"George! I'm so glad you called. How are you?" She got happy awful fast. *Who is George?*

When she got off the phone I asked her, "Was that your *boy*friend?"

She was a little embarrassed. "Well, he's a friend."

Dumb George. I'd never get Mom to think about the camping trip and all the other good family times now! How could she forget Dad so quickly?

I went to my room and emptied out two cigar boxes of seashells into a paper bag. In bright red Magic Marker I wrote MOM on the top of one box and DAD on the top of the other.

I figured since I was a two-family child, I'd better keep two "Who Am I?" boxes.

Then I took the picture of us in front of the tent and tore it in half. I put Mom and half of Mop and me in the MOM box.

And I put Dad and half of Mop and me in the DAD box.

CHAPTER THREE

Dad	Dad	Dad	Dad	Dad	Dad / Mom	Mom
19	20	21	22	23	24	25

WHEN I'M AT MOM'S I GET HOME FROM SCHOOL AT THREE-thirty, and this is what I do. First, I call my mother at her office, while Mop jumps around giving me slurpy kisses. If Mom's not in the middle of an appointment or something, we talk for a while about how school was and what we should have for supper. Then I walk Mop. Then I *eat*. I'm hungrier after school than at any other time of the day. What I like best is leftover spaghetti and sauce right out of the frig. I also like big spoonfuls of Marshmallow Fluff, peanut butter on celery, and pretzels.

While I eat I do my homework and watch TV. I *love* reruns best, like "Happy Days," "The Dick Van Dyke Show," or "The Partridge Family." The old ones are great—much funnier than the new ones. Oh yeah, and "I Love Lucy"—she's a riot.

At five my mom finishes at her office and gets ready to come home, so I turn off the TV. She says TV will turn my brain to mush. I say I'd rather have a mushy brain than die of boredom, which is what would happen to me if I didn't have television to watch after school. When I turn the TV off I turn on the radio to some good old rock 'n' roll. It keeps the spooks away when I'm in the house alone.

Then at five thirty-five my mom comes through the kitchen door and yells over the music, "I don't know how you can study with all that noise."

21

Except today she came in and said, "Where's your suitcase? Your father will be here in half an hour, and I have to be out of here in forty-five minutes."

Where's your suitcase? What kind of a hello is that? The truth is I forgot it was Friday and that I was going to my dad's.

Before Mom even took off her jacket she was rushing around my room packing everything in sight—even stuffed animals that I don't play with anymore.

"I'll do it. Just leave me alone," I told her. I shut my door and turned on my radio—real loud.

"Now hurry, Aviva. He'll be here any minute," she shouted through the door.

In the suitcase I put:

2 pair of pajamas
2 pair of jeans
1 skirt
2 sweaters
lots of socks
lots of underpants
my DAD box
1 hairbrush
1 toothbrush
Mop's brush
1 half-empty box of Mop's favorite biscuits
NO stuffed animals

"See, I told you I could do it myself," I told my mom. I took my raincoat out of the closet and put it over my arm. I got Mop's leash off the hat rack in the hall. It felt like I was going to camp all over again.

Then I sat on the suitcase in the middle of the living

room floor and watched "The Brady Bunch" while Mom took her shower.

Of course she didn't even come out and say hello to Dad when he picked me up.

Dad was in a jolly mood. He was so happy to see me it was like I was a movie star or something instead of just his kid.

His apartment looked smaller than ever now that it had some furniture in it. We ate pizza on his new kitchen table and chairs—the white metal kind that they have at sidewalk restaurants and in backyards.

"Wasn't that clever of me?" Dad grinned as he started his fourth slice of pizza.

"Dad," I said, "there's a piece of anchovy on your moustache."

He licked it off and continued, "Summer furniture is on sale because it's fall. The next time you come we'll have living room furniture."

What's that going to be, I wondered—lawn chairs?

Dad doesn't even have a TV. He got the stereo and Mom got the TV. What would I do after school when I was at Dad's?

We stuck the leftover pizza in the frig, and I went to check out my room. I put my suitcase under my new bed and sat on my new plaid bedspread. Mop jumped up on the bed and licked my face.

"You're a great-looking dog, Mop," I told him. And he is. He's got piles of gray and white hair.

We looked around. There was an old bureau next to the door. A two-shelf bookcase made with bricks and boards was under the window. Between the bed and the wall there was a small secondhand desk.

Dad came in. "Well, what do you think? Isn't this a cozy room now?"

"Fine. It's fine, Dad," I said. But I didn't smile and jump up and down and say, "Thank you. Thank you."

"Well, you unpack your clothes and toys. Then come and help me put away the kitchen stuff I got today," Dad suggested.

"But, Dad, you don't know how to cook," I reminded him.

"We'll learn." He smiled at me. "Both of us."

I looked in the empty drawers of the secondhand bureau, put my suitcase on the desk, and took out the empty cigar box with DAD written on it.

While Dad put away his new pots and pans, I looked around the kitchen for things to use on my collage. I took the part of the pizza box that said "Pizza," because I love pizza and so does Dad. Then I took one of his cigarettes. Dad says, "TV rots your brains." I say, "Cigarettes rot your lungs." And he keeps smoking and I keep watching TV.

That night Dad tucked me in like he used to when we all lived together. "We'll go grocery shopping tomorrow," he told me. "I've been waiting for you to come home to stock up. Oh, yeah, and why don't you invite your friend Sue to come stay over tomorrow night? We'll call her in the morning."

"We're not such good friends this year," I lied.

After Dad kissed me good night and turned out the light, Mop hopped on the bed and snuggled at my feet.

Loud footsteps stomping over my head. Jazzy music. Where am I? I wake up with a jump. I reach for Mop and hit my arm on the wall. My whole body

24

tightens. Where am I? Mop whimpers. Then I remember. Dad's.

Monday morning Dad dropped me off at school before he went to his teaching job at the state college. Sometimes he'll be able to pick me up after school. Not all the time, though. He says pretty soon I'll have to learn to take the bus to and from his place.

My first DAD week was just awful. I hated leaving Mop all alone in that tiny apartment without any old rugs and things to chew on. There was no TV to watch after school. My dad's a terrible cook—by Wednesday we switched to takeout. I missed mom the way I missed my dad the week before. And most of all I missed the family of Mom, Dad, me, and Mop—all together in the same house.

But the hardest thing was to keep Sue from finding out about the divorce. During recess on Tuesday she asked, "Can I come over to your house after school like we did last year?" She is the only friend Mom lets me have in the house when she's not there.

"Oh, not this week," I answered quickly.

"How come?"

"Too busy."

"Then come over to my house. Your mom will let you."

"How can I do that if I'm too busy?"

"Too busy doing what?"

"Just busy. That's all."

Sue gave me her funny wrinkled nose look. Three claps. Recess was over.

Before school on Friday Sue said, "I tried to call you after school, but nobody answered. I thought you said you were busy and couldn't play."

"That's why I wasn't there, silly. I was at the dentist."

Close calls like that all week long. I hate lying to my best friend.

And Josh was meaner and meaner to me. Since he's figured out that he can't get away with too much nonsense with Sister Bernard Marie—Cioffi calls her Sister BM behind her back—Josh picks on me all the time.

Friday afternoon, the last period, Sister pulled one of her psychological exercises on us again.

"This will help you with your collages, boys and girls. Make three lists. In the first column write ten words you think of when you think of your mother. In the second column, ten words that come to mind when you think of your father. Then in the third column, ten words that you think of when you think of yourself. Fold your paper in three columns like this." She used a blank page from Sue's notebook to demonstrate how to make three folds and then walked around the room to see if we were doing it right. I tried to fold my paper but ended up with four columns.

Josh sat there watching me. He mumbled, "Jerky turkey."

I ignored him and tried folding with a fresh piece of paper. This time I got it right.

Josh grabbed the paper from me and put his name in the right-hand corner.

By then Sister was up our aisle.

"Good, Josh, that's it." She smiled at him. She looked at the paper with four columns in front of me. "Weren't you paying attention, Aviva?" she asked.

26

"But, Sister . . ." Before I could explain, her skirts swished by my desk and she was down the aisle.

She turned to the class. "Of course if you live with only one parent, you can put anyone else you're close to in the other column."

Did she know about my parents being divorced?

I folded a new paper and looked at the three blank columns. Why doesn't Sister stick to real subjects like math and reading and geography? This isn't schoolwork. She should have been a psychiatrist instead of a nun.

At the top of the first column I wrote, "Mop." Then my list—"soft, loving, dependable, kind, loyal . . ."

Josh looked over at my paper and started writing the same words in a different order. I glared at him and covered my sheet with my arm.

Sister was still cruising the room, checking that we were doing our work. She looked at Josh's list and patted him on the back. "Good work, Josh. Your grandmother sounds like a wonderful woman."

She looked at my paper. "I don't think your dog is the first *person* you should write about, Aviva," she said.

The whole class laughed, particularly Josh. Even Sister BM thought it was pretty funny.

She clapped three times. "All right, class, that's enough. By the way, this isn't an assignment to be graded. It's to help you with your collage. Finish up now. Over the weekend try to find objects and pictures that symbolize some of the words you've written."

After school, Josh headed toward me in the schoolyard. I was ready to tell him what a jerk he was. But before I could he yelled real loud right in my face, ''Your mother's a dog, and you're a frog.''

Before I knew what I was doing, I stomped on his foot, punched him in the belly, and spit in his face—all at the same time. I didn't think about it at all. I just did it. Then I ran as fast as I could all the way home—to Mom's—without turning around once.

Mop and my suitcase were already there. Dad had dropped them off after he'd left me at school in the morning.

The phone rang as soon as I got in.

''Aviva, are you all right? Did he catch you?'' It was Sue.

''Nah, I can run faster than he can,'' I told her in my supercool voice.

''Be careful,'' Sue warned. ''Tomorrow you better come over here, maybe even sleep over. It'll be much safer.''

I let Mop out back to do his ''thing'' in the yard. Then I ran out real quick to pick it up and throw it in the garbage.

I locked the doors and closed the blinds. Mop could go for a walk later.

The phone rang again. My mom. I forgot to call her.

''You all right, honey?'' she asked. ''I missed you this week. I'm going to try to leave work early and pick up Chinese takeout for supper.'' She wasn't even mad that I forgot to call her. I didn't tell her anything about hitting Josh—or what he said.

I put both the TV and the radio on and lay back on the living room floor with my head on Mop's back and thought real hard, Josh Greene, the toes on your left foot are falling off. The toes on your right foot are falling off. Your whole right foot is falling off. . . .

By the time my mom got home from work, Josh Greene had disappeared completely—but only until Monday morning.

CHAPTER FOUR

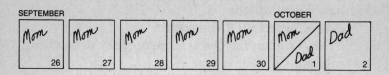

SEPTEMBER / OCTOBER

| Mom 26 | Mom 27 | Mom 28 | Mom 29 | Mom 30 | Mom / Dad 1 | Dad 2 |

I LOVE TO GO TO SUE'S HOUSE, ESPECIALLY FOR A SLEEP-over. She has a real all-American family—normal, noisy, and fun—like the Brady Bunch or the Waltons. There's always something interesting going on. Like today—her dad was raking the leaves, her brothers were shooting baskets, and her mom was making bread. They even have a "family room."

Sue and I were down there looking through old magazines for pictures to use in our "Who Am I?" collages when her mom came down the stairs arm in arm with her dad. Mrs. Crandall had on this cute blue maternity shirt that said "Baby" in big red letters with a big arrow pointing at her belly. Mr. Crandall opened the sliding doors to the yard and yelled to Sue's older brothers to come in. He had some exciting news to tell everybody.

That's another thing about their house. You feel like you're just another one of their kids when you're visiting.

The four of us sat on the couch facing Sue's parents. Mr. Crandall put his arm around Mrs. Crandall and said, "Well, your mom just got a call from the doctor. The amniocentesis test results say that our baby is A-OK."

I didn't know what an amnio-whatever test was, but everyone was real excited.

"All right!" Sue's younger brother, Tommy, shouted.

"Three cheers for our baby brother," her older brother, Alan, added.

Sue shoved him. "It's a girl."

"Don't count your chickens before they're hatched," he laughed.

"And . . ." Sue's dad quieted us down with his loud voice. He turned to Mrs. Crandall. "Well, you tell the rest, Beth."

She put her hand on her belly and announced excitedly, "The other thing the doctors could tell from the tests besides that the baby will be healthy is whether we're waiting for a boy"—she smiled at Tommy and Alan—"or a girl." She smiled at Sue and me.

That was amazing!

Her father started this long explanation about how they could tell from the fluid they took with a needle from Mrs. Crandall's womb. But no one was paying attention. We kept interrupting to ask, "What is it?"

"It's a girl, isn't it?" Sue shouted.

"Nah, it's a boy. Tell her it's a boy, Mom," Tommy interrupted.

Sue squeezed my hand. I hadn't done what she asked me to do on the first day of school. So real quick I prayed, "Please, dear God, make it a girl."

Sue's mom and dad were having fun making us wait to find out. Finally her mom began, "It's . . ."

"Tell us, tell us. Hurry up."

"It's a . . . *girl!*"

Everyone—even me—went crazy. It was such a happy day in that house. They decided to make a surprise party for the baby girl, even though she was still inside her mother. They invited Sue's grandparents and some of the neighbors.

There were discussions all day long about what they should call her. Sue said she should be able to name the baby because she was the other girl in the family. Her father said they just might name her Mildred Gertrude after both her grandmothers!

Sue and I helped her mom make salads for the cookout. Mrs. Crandall put her arm around me. "Aviva, why don't we invite your parents to help us celebrate. I'll call them. You know, our two families have never gotten together outside of school. It's about time, don't you think?"

"They're busy," I blurted out. "Going to a party." In a way it was the truth because my mom was going out with George Whats-his-name and my dad was bound to be busy, too.

"Wish I had thought of it earlier," Mrs. Crandall said. "Well, at least we have you." And she showed me how to use the Cuisinart to chop up the cabbage and carrots. It made enough coleslaw for fifteen people in two minutes flat.

Nobody noticed how quiet I was at the barbecue. They were too busy being a family and having a great time naming that baby girl. I watched the whole scene and pretended they were a TV family. It'd make a terrific series: "The Crandall Clan." I thought about which stars could play the parts and what some of the different episodes could be about. This one would be "A Party for Whats-Her-Name." There sure wasn't any room for a two-family child with divorced parents in a show like that.

When we got into bed Sue was still chattering on about the baby. She wanted to name her Nicole.

"Since Nicole is going to be born at Christmastime," Sue reasoned, "I'm going to put a picture of a pine tree on my collage and decorate it with pink ribbons—real ones. Want to help me?"

"Sure," I mumbled. I turned over so she wouldn't know I was crying. It was a long time before I floated, floated, floated, then sank into sleep.

Sunday at Mom's was just the opposite of Saturday at Sue's. It was quiet, lonely, and boring. Since my mom works all week, she spent most of the day cleaning and cooking. I helped—a little. I picked up my room, did the wash, and brushed Mop. Then I started my homework.

The first thing was to look for some objects for my MOM box. I took a pair of chopsticks out of the kitchen drawer because we have Chinese takeout at least once a week. And I got a piece of red yarn from the basket near the couch because Mom's been knitting me the same red mittens for the past two years.

She stopped vacuuming and watched me put the things in the MOM box. "Aviva, you should collect more things about *you* for the collage. I have just the thing. Come on."

I followed her into her bedroom. She poked through the clothes in her bottom drawer. "Do you believe this?" She laughed as she held up the tiniest undershirt I'd ever seen, with little pink rosebuds all over it.

"It's real cute, Mom," I told her, "but I don't play with dolls anymore."

"But it's not dolls' clothes. It was yours. This was your very first undershirt. You wore it home from the hospital. When I gave your other baby clothes away I

34

just couldn't part with this. Why don't you use it on your collage?'' She had tears in her eyes. ''You were the world's best baby.''

But I didn't feel sappy or sentimental at all. I was angry. ''You know what, Mom,'' I said real loud. ''Remember when I came home from camp and you and Dad said you had something important to tell me? I thought you were going to say you were having a baby. But you didn't. You told me about getting divorced.''

Mom's face turned sad, which was just what I wanted. I went into my room until supper.

That little shirt was even too small for my Snoopy. I thought about what Mom said about using it on my collage. So I took my scissors and cut it in half—half for my MOM box and half for my DAD box. Then I put my boxes away.

I had had quite enough of babies for one weekend.

Then I remembered Josh. He came back—toes, feet, legs, body, arms, head—just the way he'd be in school on Monday. Rip-roaring mad at me and looking for revenge.

I sat on my bed, looking over my homework assignments to see what else I had to do, when I realized that I'd left my first big history assignment at my dad's and it was due the next day. That's when I got an idea that could solve part of my Josh problem and help get my parents back together at the same time. I'd get Mom to go to Dad's place with me before school to pick up my history paper.

I figured it this way. When Mom saw how little and pathetic Dad's apartment was she might invite him to move back in with us. And when Dad saw how pretty Mom's been looking lately with her new haircut he was sure to fall in love with her all over again. They'd sit at his silly little outdoor furniture in the kitchen area, and I would wait in my bedroom while they made up over a cup of coffee. And if Mom brought me to Dad's to get my homework, I would be late for school and not have to worry about Josh until recess. Besides, if my parents made up, we all might take the day off to celebrate and I wouldn't have to go to school at all.

Monday morning I put my plan into action. Mom was washing the breakfast dishes, and I was packing my lunch and books.

"Oh, no, Mom," I moaned. "I left my history paper at Dad's, and I have to hand it in today."

"Explain it to Sister. I'm sure she'll understand." Mom didn't even turn around. "Your dad can drop it off tonight. With two houses you just have to be more organized, Aviva."

"Please, Mom," I pleaded. "You've got to drive me over to Dad's before you go to work. Sister'll kill me. I'll get an F! You don't want me to get off to a bad start in school, do you?"

Mom's shoulders slumped the way they do when she's about to give in to me. "All right. I guess it'll take you a while to get used to this back and forth business." She turned around and gave me a weak smile. "It must be hard to keep your things straight."

I gave her my saddest "poor me" look. "Yeah, it is." That was sure to get her.

"I'll bring you to Dad's, then to school, and . . . I'll be late for work."

"I'll write you a late note," I offered.

She didn't laugh.

When we pulled up in front of my dad's building, Mom double-parked the car and told me to hurry up.

"Aren't you going to come with me?" I asked.

36

"Aviva, you're almost eleven years old. Now hurry up."

"But—"

"Now!" My mom's "nows" are like Sister Bernard Marie's claps. Final.

"Nice building," Mom commented as I was getting out of the car.

I bent my head back in the car window. "No it's not. New buildings are poorly constructed. The walls are thin. And Dad's apartment is real tiny. Why don't you come see?"

Mom growled, "Aviva, go! *Now.*"

The superintendent in Dad's building was running the elevator. He gives me the creeps. He's always looking at you over his glasses and rolling cigarettes.

"Ninth floor," I told him.

He nudged his glasses lower on his nose and looked at me. "You're Mr. Granger's kid. Right? The divorced guy in 9D?"

I mumbled yes but didn't smile at him or anything. *What business is it of his?*

When we got to the ninth floor he said, "Well, have a nice day." I hate it when people you don't even know say, "Have a nice day." Especially when you know you're *not* going to have a nice day at all, that in fact you're going to have a crummy day.

I took out the key to 9D. At least it would be fun to surprise my dad. His apartment is so small that as soon as you open the front door you're in the kitchen/living room/dining room all at once. But I was in the wrong apartment. A blond lady was making coffee in the kitchen.

"Sorry," I blurted out. "Wrong apartment."

The key worked, I suddenly realized. And the kitchen furniture is just like Dad's.

"You're Aviva," she said.

How does she know my name?

"I saw your picture. Come on in."

What picture?

She called toward the bathroom, "Roy, your daughter's here."

"What?" Dad came rushing into the room with shaving cream over half his face and his razor in his hand.

"What are you doing here?" He sounded angry, then scared. "Has something happened? Is Jan all right?"

"I . . . my history . . ." I didn't look at the blonde again—not once—just at my dad and my red sneakers. "I forgot my history paper. It's in my desk. I'll get it."

What if Mom decided to come up after all? If she found out about the blonde, my parents would never, ever get back together.

I dashed into my room and grabbed my paper from the top drawer. Dad was following me, still half-soaped, still holding his razor. "Aviva, slow down. I want to introduce you to Vivian. She's a friend of mine. I've been wanting you to meet her."

"Can't." I brushed past him. "Late for school."

I ran out the door and down the nine flights of stairs. I didn't want Dad and that woman following me to the elevator, and I certainly didn't want to see the super again.

I jumped into the car. "Let's go," I said.

Mom started the motor up and turned to me.

"That was fast. I said hurry, not fly. Here, have a donut."

She shoved a bag of sugar donuts across the seat. "You and Roy have a great bakery across the street and a nice big grocery store. That's real convenient. He's found a good spot." What she said was friendly enough, but her tone wasn't. I wondered if she knew about the blond lady too.

The greasy smell of the donuts made me want to puke. I pushed the bag back to Mom. "No thanks."

When we got to school Mom and I wrote late notes for each other. She said her boss would get a kick out of it, because she had kids too. All the time we were writing the notes, I had a picture in my head of my dad with shaving cream over half his face kissing the blond lady. When I walked through the doors of St. Agnes's, the image of a mean, angry Josh pushed the blonde and Daddy right out of my mind.

I handed Sister my note and walked slowly up the aisle of room 410B toward my seat in the last row. Josh didn't even look up at me. Maybe I really hurt him and he is afraid of *me* for a change. Maybe my troubles in the back of the room are over.

There was a note on my desk. From Sue?

I opened my English book to the page Sister told me and slipped the note behind it. Sue's family probably had decided on a name for their baby, and she wanted to tell me right away.

I opened it.

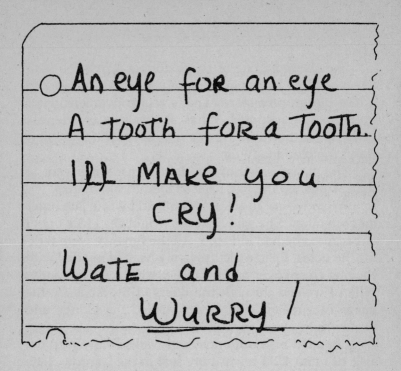

An eye for an eye
A tooth for a tooth.
Ill MAKE you
CRY!

WATE and
WURRY!

I looked out of the corners of my eyes at Josh. He had one lanky leg stretched out in each aisle. His blond hair was as messy as ever. He looked straight ahead, listening to Sister Bernard Marie like he was her prize pupil.

At recess Sue and I rushed into the girls' room before everyone else.

"You better tell Sister what happened," Sue said.

In the mirror I saw Janet, Rita, and Louise coming in.

"Shh." I grabbed the note from Sue and stuck it in my pocket. "Don't say anything."

They crowded around us, all talking at once.

"We were so scared when you weren't here this morning."

"What do you think he's going to do?"

"You must be awful worried."

"Cioffi told me you better watch out, Aviva. He said Josh is *real* mad."

I gave Sue a "don't-dare-tell" look, swallowed back my fear, brushed back my hair with my hands, then announced calmly, "I don't think he'll do anything."

"I do," blurted Janet. "Josh has a knife. You should have a bodyguard."

"Or police protection," added Louise.

"Yeah," they all agreed.

"Well, I'm not afraid of Josh Greene," I said as I crumpled his note deeper into my pocket, "knife or no knife."

Then I went to the yard with Sue and hung around Sister for the rest of recess.

I was the first one out of the classroom after school. I ran the whole way home instead of waiting for the bus.

"Mop needs a good run," my mother told me when I called to say I was home. "Take him to the park and pick up my order at the butcher's."

It was a pretty fall day—crisp and blue. Just the opposite of how I felt—limp and gray. The idea of walking around the neighborhood with Josh Greene after me was so frightening that I ate four tablespoons of Marshmallow Fluff before we left.

Once I got outdoors with Mop, though, I wasn't afraid at all. I did have a bodyguard. Mop wouldn't let anyone hurt me—no way! If only I could take him to school.

But I didn't see any sign of Josh that afternoon, and

he didn't do anything to me at school that week either. By Wednesday everyone in our class seemed to have forgotten that I had beat him up. Everybody except me.

The weirdest thing was that Josh didn't even tease me or copy off my papers. And when he fooled around with Cioffi behind Sister's back, it was as if I didn't exist or had been transferred to another class. Actually it was becoming pretty boring for me in the back of the room.

Then on Friday I found this note in my lunch pail.

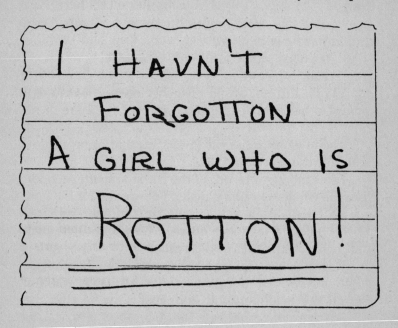

I HAVN'T FORGOTTON A GIRL WHO IS ROTTON!

Friday, after my daily TV shows, Mop and I packed up to go back to Dad's. "Seems like we just got here and we're packing again," I complained to Mop as I pulled my suitcase out from my closet.

I sat on my bed and looked around my room. I love it—clutter, clutter, clutter. I collect seashells and stuffed animals and detective stories and anything that has rainbows on it. I have rainbow soap, rainbow pillows, strips of seven different kinds of rainbow stickers. My collection of fifteen rainbow greeting cards is on the wall over my desk. Rainbows with hearts, unicorns, musical notes, cats, and a preppy rainbow with an alligator in the corner.

When Mom came home from work she handed me my toothbrush and hairbrush to pack. "Leave these at Dad's," she said. "I'll get you another set for here. Next week we'll buy some extra underwear and pajamas so you won't have to bring everything back and forth."

"What about Mop's brush?" I asked.

"We'll get another brush for Mop too. Now hurry up. I'm meeting someone at seven o'clock, and I have to drop you off at Dad's on the way."

"Who?" I asked.

"Who what?"

"Who are you meeting?"

"A friend."

"Your *boy*friend?"

My mother blushed and started this silly talk about how wonderful George was and how she wanted me to meet him. She was sounding like the high school girls at St. Agnes's who gossip about boys all during lunch hour. It was really ridiculous. I just sat there staring at her. There was nothing I could say.

Finally she changed the subject. "Well." She looked around at my beloved clutter. "Aviva, why don't you take half of this stuff for your room at Roy's. It'll make it homier for you. After all, you live there half the time."

"Nah." I jumped off my bed, opened my suitcase, and started throwing my clothes in. "I can't be bothered. Besides, I told you, the apartment is very small. There isn't room for a lot of stuff.''

Inside I said, How can you fall in love with anybody but Dad? Please don't. Please, please, please don't. Just ask Dad to come home so we can be a family again.

CHAPTER FIVE

Dad	Dad	Dad	Dad	Dad	Dad / Mom	Mom
3	4	5	6	7	8	9

ACTUALLY DAD'S APARTMENT HAD LOTS OF NEW STUFF IN IT without me bringing anything extra. There was a new navy blue couch with a pattern of little white flowers and a round braided rug in front of that. His books were out of the cardboard boxes and lined up neatly on new bookshelves. He had even put up white lace curtains in the windows.

Dad put his arm around me and gave me a big hug. "Good to have you back, pumpkin." He looked over the room. "What do you think?"

Mop sprawled out on the rug in front of the couch and looked up at me with his "this-isn't-a-bad-life-for-a-dog" look. It was really good to see my dad without soap on his face and a blonde at his side.

"Nice," I admitted.

"Now go see what's in your bedroom."

I started toward my room, which is only about ten steps. Mop scrambled off the rug past me. He always thinks I'm racing him, even when I'm not. He won.

My window had a new yellow curtain, and there was a small TV on top of my bureau.

"Yippee!" I shouted. Mop and I jumped all over Dad thanking him.

"I thought your brain might as well rot evenly," he explained. "Just follow the same TV rules that you have at Jan's." (Which means "Don't let me know how much TV you watch, and your grades better not go down.")

He turned on the TV so I could see how good the re-

45

ception was. ''Vivian gave it to you. She said she hardly watches it, so you might as well use it. She doesn't let her kids watch TV at all. Great kids. You'll meet them all sometime soon and you can thank Vivian for the TV yourself.''

The blonde! What a creep she must be, I thought. She doesn't even let her kids watch TV. She's probably the reason my parents are getting divorced. I'll never, ever talk to her, I decided. And my dad can just forget about thank-you's.

I didn't watch *any* TV that night.

The next morning, as we were eating cold leftover pizza for breakfast, Dad and I decided we'd better learn how to cook. We made out our menu for the weekend—spaghetti, french toast, hamburgers—simple stuff to start.

While Dad corrected his papers, I went across the street to the shopping center to buy the ingredients.

I could see Dad was going to need more than a little help with this housekeeping business, and if I didn't help him the blond lady would.

I tied Mop's leash to a parking meter and gave him two biscuits to munch on and went in. It was fun to zip around the aisles deciding what kind of this and what kind of that to buy. From the checkout counter I could see that Mop was having a grand time too, playing with some kid. I couldn't tell if it was a girl or boy because of all the This Week's Specials signs in the window. What I could tell was that Mop was having fun. I love it when people pay attention to him. Mop's real special and very popular. If I could trade Mop for Sue's new baby sister, I wouldn't. Sometimes I think I love my dog even more

46

than I love my parents. Animals are much more dependable than people.

As I was coming out of the store with my groceries I moved aside to let a woman with two carts overflowing with groceries go ahead of me. With the door opened I could hear an old lady saying to the kid, "Dogs are too much trouble, and they cost a lot to feed."

"Not so, Nana," a boy's voice answered. "Besides, I can get a job after school to pay for it."

"If you make some money, boy," she said, "we need it to feed us. Now stop your dreaming."

Some kids have it tough, I thought, until I got out of the store and saw that the boy playing with Mop was Josh Greene!

What if he had his knife? I dropped my packages and ran over and pulled Josh away from Mop.

"Don't you dare touch my dog," I shouted.

Josh grabbed my arm and twisted it behind me and faced me squarely. "Hey, I didn't even know it was your dog. Besides, I'm not after your dog, turkey. I'm after *you*."

Mop growled at Josh and pulled on his leash. The old lady started screaming at Josh to let me go. "My heart," she cried to Josh. He let go of me and went over to her.

"Come on, Grandma," he said, "you better sit down."

He led her toward the little park around the corner. She was yelling, "She's crazy. That girl's crazy. See what having a dog does to you."

Mop started whimpering for me to untie him. I felt angry and silly at the same time, especially when I saw that the super from my dad's building was standing in front of the market watching me over his glasses and laughing at the whole scene.

He helped me pick up my groceries, and he insisted on carrying one of my packages across the street to our building.

"You been with your dad a lot," he commented while we waited for the light. "You're not moving in with him or anything, are you?"

"I live with my dad half the time," I told him. He gave me a funny look as we crossed the street, like he'd never heard of that before or didn't know what "half the time" meant.

"Every other week I live with my dad," I explained.

"And you always have that dog with you?"

"Yeah. He's my dog. He goes wherever I go."

I pulled Mop's leash to bring him closer to me as we went into the building.

"You telling me that you and that dog live here half the time?" the super asked as he handed me my package.

Boy was he dense. "Yeah, with my dad."

"Well, it's okay for you to live here, but not the dog. No dogs allowed in this building—whole time or half time. Kids are bad enough. You tell your father to check his lease."

He got on the service elevator. As the doors were closing he shouted, "Don't let me see that dog in this building again."

Mop growled. I stood there for a second staring at the closed elevator door.

Instead of waiting for the passenger elevator, I ran up the nine flights of stairs, groceries and all. Mop kept up with me, dragging his leash—clink-clank—all the way. "Don't worry, Mop," I told him. "We'll just move out of his dumb old building. Dad'll take care of it."

When we got to the apartment I knocked on the door with my foot and yelled, "Dad!" Mop barked.

"Hold it. I'm coming," Dad called.

He opened the door. Mop bolted right to his spot on the rug, and I just stood there in the hall trying to tell the whole story at once. "Dad, Dad, we've got to move out of this place right away!"

My dad sat me down on the couch and had me tell him what happened slowly, step by step.

When I finished the whole story he said, "I was afraid this might happen. I hoped Mr. Summers would look the other way about Mop since you're only here half the time." He rubbed Mop's back with his foot. "Look, Aviva, I'll talk to him, but I doubt he's going to bend."

"Then we'll just have to move!" I shouted at him. "We'll show him."

But Dad didn't agree with me. He said we just got here and we weren't going to move again. Besides, it cost a lot of money to move, and it's hard to find a place. "We aren't moving just because of Mop, Aviva," he finished.

"You found this apartment. You can find another one," I shouted.

"Aviva!" he said sharply. When my dad says "Aviva!" like that, it means the same thing as when my mom says "Now!" or Sister Bernard Marie claps three times.

I sat on the couch. Mop put his head on my lap, and I braided the hair around his ears while Dad went to talk to Mr. Summers.

Only half the time with Mop! I couldn't, I wouldn't, live like that. Mop looked up at me and whimpered. He definitely knew something was wrong.

Dad came in and sat in a plump on the couch next to me. "Mr. Summers said Mop can stay this weekend and that's it. Monday we'll have to bring him to your mom's. I'm sorry, honey, there's nothing I can do."

Well, I didn't do anything, either, for the whole rest of the day. I just stretched out on my bed with Mop and thought about how much I hated the super and the divorce and joint custody and Josh Greene. Lying there thinking, I got the idea that maybe Mop's getting kicked out of Dad's building might bring my parents back together. Didn't it prove how ridiculous this divorce business was? Look at all the trouble it was causing Mop and me.

I opened my door so I could listen when my dad called my mom. But all he talked about was when he would drop Mop off on Monday and how sad it was to separate Mop and me but there was nothing he could do about it. And when Mom talked to me on the phone she said all the same things Dad had said. Then she tried to change the subject to my Halloween/birthday party and said how we would pick out invitations when I came back in a week. I didn't care about any old party. I didn't care about any anything except keeping Mop and me together.

Dad planned to drop Mop off at my mom's after he picked me up from school. We would get Mop from the apartment, walk him, and bring him to 110 Elm Street, where he'd stay all the time from then on.

That was Dad's plan. My plan was different.

Monday morning I told him he wouldn't have to go out of his way anymore to drop me off at school. I was ready to take the bus.

Dad got in the car to go to work, and I got on the bus, but not to go to school. After the bus had gone a few blocks and I was sure Dad was on his way, I got off and ran back to the apartment.

Mop jumped up and licked my face he was so glad to have me come back right away. "Don't worry, Mop," I told him, "they can't break us up. Let's get ready to go out on our own."

I found some of the things I needed in the back of Dad's closet shelf—a backpack, a canteen, a waterproof ground cover, a flashlight, and a Swiss army knife.

From the kitchen I got matches, dog food, dried fruits and nuts, cheese, crackers, peanut butter, and oranges. I put them in a knapsack with a clean T-shirt, sweater, warm socks, and underpants. I filled the canteen with fresh water, and I took the twenty-five dollars my uncle Ben sent me from California last Christmas from the pocket in my suitcase.

Mop and I locked up and left.

We went down the back stairs so no one would see us, but on the last flight we bumped into the last person in the world I wanted to see just then—the super. Before he could say anything to me I shouted, "He *is* leaving. Right now. I hope you're satisfied, you mean old jackass." Mop gave out his most ferocious bark and we stormed out of the building.

I knew just where to go. There are woods that start about a mile from my dad's, a terrific pine forest that marks the edge of our town and goes on for at least ten miles to the next town.

I know all about living in the woods from camping with my mom and dad and from sleep-away camp. In August our camp group lived in the wild for three days with hardly any supplies, not even a tent.

It was a wonderful morning. The woods were dark green and brown, the sky clear blue. Mop was off his leash and running wild. I was independent and free—free of my dumb parents, who didn't even love me and Mop enough to get along with each other and make a real family; free of my school, with stupid, mean Josh and dumb assignments like "Who Am I?" collages.

I knew who I was. I was Aviva Granger, and I could take care of myself and my dog.

After a couple of hours we turned off the trail. I blazed the way by marking the trees with small slashes so we could find our way back if we needed to. When the sun was directly overhead, we stopped for lunch.

I found a clearing. Mop munched his dog biscuits and I ate peanut butter on crackers and an orange. Then we just lay back and watched puffy white clouds glide across the sky.

We'd be okay. We had enough food for three days and twenty-five dollars to buy more in the next town. I knew which wild plants were edible. When it got colder we could still manage. I knew how to build shelters, make fires—even without a match—and stuff my clothes with dried leaves to keep warm.

We didn't need anybody—no Dad, no Mom, no school. I put my head on Mop and took a nap.

When I woke up it was late afternoon. I looked up at the sun moving toward the west. School would be just about getting out.

I could just see it now.

Dad is waiting for me at school. When I don't show up he thinks I took the bus or had to stay after. Sue sees the car and asks him what he's doing there, since I wasn't even in school. He rushes back to his apartment—no me, no Mop. Was I kidnapped from the bus? He calls my mom at her office. She starts crying on the phone and says she'll be right there. Dad asks around the building if anyone saw me after eight-thirty that morning. The super says that Mop and I left together and I had a backpack. Dad hits him hard right on the jaw for all the trouble he's caused. Now Dad knows I ran away. Mom comes to his apartment. They both cry and make up.

"What have we done? She's left us, Roy," my mom says.

"Yes." My father puts his arm around her. "It was our fault. How foolish we were. If only our little girl would come home."

Maybe I would . . . some day.

Mop and I had a snack and walked a little deeper into the woods, still marking our trail on the bark of the pine trees. When I figured we were about halfway to the next town I set up our campsite for the night.

It didn't look like rain, but I made a lean-to shelter with the ground cover and some branches. Even though I had matches, I made a fire without them just for practice. There wasn't much else to do in the woods.

Mop poked around near our campsite but always came running when I called his name.

It got cooler as it got darker. We huddled together near the fire. I sang some of the songs I learned at camp.

> Rise up old flame
> By the light growing
> Show to us beauty, wisdom, and joy.

My voice sounded very small in the forest.

"You know what, Mop?" I asked.

He barked.

"I wish you could speak English."

He wagged his tail.

Then I sort of dozed off. There wasn't anything else to do.

I'm floating on a cloud with my mom, Dad, and Mop. The cloud splits in two pieces. Dad is on one piece. Mom is on the other. Mop and I are on a splinter of cloud that's left when the cloud splits. We fall off the edge of this little bit of fluff and fall through the sky. I cry out to my parents. They reach over the edge of their cloud-islands, but I'm falling, falling. I cry, "Daddy, Mommy, help me." I try to grab on to Mop, but he is out of reach too as I sink alone through the air. Mop barks for help and I cry.

I was crying when I woke up. I could still hear Mop's pained barks, but I couldn't see anything. The fire had gone out, and it had become pitch black dark while I was sleeping. I sat up and rubbed my eyes. I tried to shake my bad dream. But Mop was crying for real, not just in my dream. Where was he? What was wrong?

I found the flashlight in the bottom of my backpack and searched our campsite with its narrow band of light in the direction of Mop's barks.

Has Mop been injured?

Is he holding a wild animal at bay?

Is a bear about to grab me?

With the beam of light I picked up Mop under a pine tree. He was barking and scratching at his left hip.

I went over and got him to stay still long enough for me to look at his hip. Under the fur I saw a few small black spots about the size of tacks. Thorns? "It's okay, Mop," I comforted him. "Stay still and I'll get them out."

I grabbed one between my fingernails and pulled. I couldn't get it out, and it moved—deeper into Mop. It wasn't a thorn, it was some kind of bug, burying itself in the flesh. Mop barked and barked and wouldn't let me try to get it out again.

"Let me help you!" I cried. He scratched his other hip and then his neck.

In the four years I had my dog I'd never seen him so miserable. There was nothing I could do . . . and there was no one I could ask for help. Horrible bugs all over Mop, maybe infecting him with poison or even eating him alive!

I might be able to survive in the woods, but I wasn't doing a very good job of taking care of my dog. I had to get help.

I moved around the campsite in the dark, packing up our stuff. When I had it all together and was sure there weren't any embers left in our campfire, I went over to Mop.

"Come on, Mop, let's go," I coaxed. He yelped and scratched and wouldn't leave.

I tried one more time to pull out the bugs, but Mop yelped and snarled so, that I had to stop. Finally I leashed him and practically dragged him behind me through the woods.

Each time I stopped to flash my light along the trees to find our blazed trail of notches Mop would stop to scratch and whine.

How would I ever get him home?

CHAPTER SIX

IT WAS THE DARKEST NIGHT EVER. NO MOON. NO STARS. Just pitch black. I had spent nights in the dark woods before. But I was always with my parents or with kids at camp. We were all together and we had fun. Besides, we mostly slept during the dark nights. Now I was awake and alone, moving through the woods with a sick dog.

After about twenty-thousand hours there were no more slashes on the trees. We reached the regular trail. Now I wouldn't have to stop every few yards to look for our marks on the bark.

I poured water from my canteen into the palm of my hand and held it out for Mop to drink. After about ten handfuls he stopped drinking and went back to scratching.

I beamed the flashlight straight ahead and gritted my teeth. "Mop Granger," I said in an army sergeant voice, "this is it!" I ran, pulling on Mop's leash as hard as I could so he'd have no choice but to stop scratching and keep up with me.

We ran twenty paces, then walked twenty. Run twenty. Walk twenty. During the twenty walking paces I chanted out loud to keep up my courage.

> Left. Left. Left my wife and forty-two kids,
> An old gray mare and a TV too.
> Did I do right? Right.
> Right. Left. Right.
> Hayfoot, strawfoot, shift by jingle.
> Left. Left. Left my wife . . .

An owl hooted. Our flashlight made eerie patterns of

light on the bushes along the trail. The trees were huge monsters looming overhead; their branches became arms with a million fingers about to grab us and hurl us through the inky sky.

This was most definitely the scariest night of my life.

Run twenty. Walk twenty.

> Left. Left. Left my mother and father too.
> Did I do right? Right.
> Right. Left. Right.
> Hayfoot, strawfoot, shift by jingle.
> Left. Left. Left my mother and father too.
> Did I do right?

Run twenty. Walk twenty. Follow the beam of light. Don't look up at the monster trees. Keep to the trail. One foot after the other. Mile after mile.

Suddenly the brush along the trail was looking dark green instead of black. I looked up. The outlines of the trees against the sky were more distinct. Was it already dawn?

I stood on a big rock and looked all around. Squinting through the tree branches I saw the white glow of streetlamps and could make out red letters: E . . . X. The Exxon station at the shopping center near Dad's.

"Come on, Mop," I shouted. "We made it!" No more counting. We just ran until we were out of the woods. Poor Mop. He yelped and lay down—right there on a patch of soft grass near the A&P—and wouldn't budge. I tied his leash to a tree and ran the rest of the way to Dad's. I'd get help for Mop.

I rang Dad's doorbell. I stood there, dirty, scratched

up. The flashlight dangled from my hand, making a tiny moving circle of light on the hallway tiles.

My mother opened the door. "Oh, God!" she cried. "Aviva!" She pulled me close to her chest. "Thank God you're all right!"

I pulled away from her. "Mop, Mop. Something awful's happened to Mop. Do something," I shouted.

Dad was right behind my mom. "Dad," I pleaded, "Mop's sick at the shopping center. Help me."

On the elevator all three of us were crying. Mom and Dad because they were so glad I was back and okay. And me because I was so scared about Mop.

In the car Dad said, "Sounds like Mop has ticks. They're tough to get out, but not impossible."

Mop was huddled where I left him, scratching away. I held his paws while Mom parted his fur and Dad trained the flashlight beam on the bugs.

"Just what I thought," my dad observed, "ticks."

Mop got in the backseat with me and we all drove over to Mom's, where we wouldn't have to worry about the dumb old super.

We got Mop to lie down on Mom's living room rug. I held his paws and talked soothing things to him like, "You're such a good dog. . . . It's going to be all right, Mop. . . . Everything's just fine."

The way to get ticks out is to put a lit match on the part of the tick that's showing. The heat makes it loosen its grip so you can pull it out.

As Dad took the first tick out Mop snarled and tried to bite my arm, so Dad held his jaws closed. I found the ticks and parted the fur so it wouldn't burn and Mom did the light-heat-pull job.

This is what a tick looks like. Gray and round, some were almost as big as a dime and *filled* with Mop's blood.

This is what you have to do after you take the ticks out. Squash them dead.

This is how many ticks there were in Mop. Thirty-one! Yech.

"You were very smart to get Mop out of those woods," Dad told me as I applied alcohol to the bites the ticks had left on Mop's skin. "If Mop had been bitten on the spine, he could have gotten tick paralysis."

When Dad let Mop's jaws free, he ran over to the TV set and tried to hide under the stand.

"My poor Mop," I said as I plopped exhausted on the couch. He looked up at me from under his big paw. "We had to do it that way," I explained. "We were helping you. Now don't you feel better?" He looked at me with those big sad brown eyes. "Come on, Mop," I pleaded. "I love you. I'm sorry I took you with me into the woods."

He got up, lumbered over to the couch, and put his head in my lap. We fell asleep right there, just like that.

Big slurpy kisses and hungry growls woke me up around ten o'clock. We went into the kitchen. Mom was sitting there in her bathrobe sipping coffee. "Hi, sleepy," she greeted me. "I'm not going to work today." I bent over to give her a good-morning kiss. She smiled at me. "No school for you either. We all need a good rest."

I had a huge breakfast, took a bubble bath, put on my pajamas, and went right back to bed and slept all afternoon. So did Mop.

When I woke up I watched "Gilligan's Island." Gilligan and the captain and Mary Ann seemed to be having a great time living away from civilization and horsing around. Well, that sure wasn't the way it was for Mop and me.

A chill went through my body as I remembered being alone in the woods. Well, at least we didn't get lost, I thought. And the truth was that if Mop hadn't gotten messed up with ticks, we'd probably still be there eating oranges and peanut butter and being very bored.

At five o'clock I heard my dad's car pull in the driveway. I guessed it was time for me to go back to his place since it was still a DAD week. Mop would just have to stay with Mom. There was nothing I could do about that.

I went to the front hall to meet Dad. He had my suitcase with him. Were we all going to live together again?

"Aviva," my mom said when she met Dad and me in the hall. "Dad and I want to talk to you. Let's all go to the kitchen."

I followed them in and sat at the table. Mom poured coffee for herself and Dad and gave me a glass of orange juice. This is it, I thought. Maybe running away wasn't such a bad idea after all.

"Listen, we did a lot of thinking and talking while you were in the woods," my mom began.

Here it comes. They're going to tell me how they're getting back together. How they know now that the whole divorce business was a horrible mistake. That we all belong together—a family.

"And," my Dad continued, "we think this going back and forth business is too difficult for you right now. Your running away proves that."

He looked at me sadly, then at my mom. "We both feel it would be better for you to live here most of the time. At least for now. We all have to think about this equal time business and do what's best for you, Aviva."

"You mean you're not going to move back here, Dad?" I pleaded with my biggest sad-eyed look.

"No. That's not going to happen," my mom said. Then the two of them launched into their old "it's-not-your-fault-darling-but-we're-not-getting-back-to-gether-again" speech, which they had been giving me since the divorce began.

"I'm still real tired," I interrupted them. "I think I'll go back to bed."

I did. And slept until it was time for school the next day.

"Please excuse Aviva from school this past Monday and Tuesday. Her absence was unavoidable."

I love my mom's notes. She never says stuff like "Aviva missed school last week because she had the flu" or "Aviva was out of school yesterday because she had a dentist appointment." Just: "Her absence was unavoidable."

I saw a note on Mr. Campbell's desk last year from Rita's mother. Perfect handwriting on dainty paper with a border of little red roses announced, "Rita didn't go to school on Wednesday because she had a severe case of diarrhea." Cripes.

I hoped Sister wouldn't ask me why I was absent.

Finally she closed the note and looked up at me from her desk. "See me at recess. I'll give you the assignments you missed." Then she looked toward the back of the room. "Josh, would you please give Aviva your history notes to copy over while I take attendance."

Josh!

I caught Sue's eye as I headed toward my seat. She

shook her head in sympathy while the rest of the class giggled.

Three claps. By the time I got to my seat, Sister was scolding, "Josh's history notes are just as good as anybody else's. Now quiet down."

Sister didn't even know what the kids were laughing about. She didn't know that Josh was a class-A creep who'd been terrorizing me since the first grade. Teachers can be so dumb—even nuns.

Josh grinned his most evil "just-wait-until-I-get-you" smirk as he handed me a pile of papers folded in half.

"Now," Sister continued, "the rest of you look over your English homework while I take attendance."

I figured the way that Josh did his schoolwork, his notes would be pretty useless. I'd just have to get them from Sue during lunch hour.

I opened the papers he handed me. Gooey, disgusting *Spit* dripped from a scribbled note: "Too scared to come to school, turkey?"

I was so mad! "No, jerk," I scribbled on a dry corner of the page. "I went on a trip!"

I shoved the whole mess on his desk—spitside down.

When Cioffi saw the spit all over Josh's desk he hooted his silly loud laugh.

"Mr. Cioffi!" Sister looked up from her desk. "Change places with Sue for the day. We'll see if you find it as amusing in the front of the room."

"But, I didn't . . ." Cioffi tried to protest.

"*Mr.* Cioffi. *No* buts, just *move.*"

And he did.

While everyone was distracted watching long-legged Cioffi scrunching into Sue's short desk, Josh crumpled the pages of spit into a ball and threw the world's biggest spitball back on my desk.

I brushed it off with my notebook and watched it roll under his chair. He kicked it back under mine.

I left it there. Sue was sitting in the seat next to me. Josh Greene could spit himself dry, for all I cared.

CHAPTER SEVEN

Mom 10	Mom 11	Mom 12	Mom 13	Mom 14	Mom / Dad 15	Dad 16

"I'M SORT OF SICK OF RAINBOWS, MOM. I THINK I'VE OUT-grown them." I wrinkled my nose at her. "You know what I mean?"

"Oh, I see," she said as she replaced a pack of invitations with rainbow-colored letters demanding, "Come To My Party."

"I like these better," I told her. They were *real* Halloween party invitations, with a witch riding a broomstick past a full moon.

We did our grocery shopping and picked Sue up at her house on the way home.

Sue and I made ourselves a pound of elbow macaroni, loaded it with butter, salt, and pepper, and ate it while we made a list of sixteen kids from our class that would get invitations to my party.

Then we sat on my bed and wrote out the answers to the questions on the cards.

WHAT? *A Party*

WHEN? *October 30th at 6:00 P.M.*

WHERE? *110 Elm Street*

WHO—OO—OO? *Avira Granger*

65

"Well, that's it," I said as I sealed the last envelope.

Sue slapped herself on the cheek. "I don't believe who we forgot, Aviva."

"Who?"

"Just the most important friend you have!" she cried.

I looked over the list one more time. We had checked off each name as we addressed the envelopes. There were sixteen names and sixteen envelopes.

"Who did I forget?" I asked again.

"I really can't believe you'd forget somebody that's such a good friend."

I threw my pillow at her. "Who? You better tell me."

"Think hard," she teased.

"Sue Crandall," I threatened. "If you don't tell me—and fast—I'll throw you in the shower." (There are some advantages to being much taller than your best friend.)

She threw the pillow back at me. "Think hard."

"You asked for it." I ran around the bed, picked her up like she was four years old, and carried her kicking and laughing into the bathroom. Then I plopped her in the tub and held her with one hand while I reached for the cold water faucet with the other.

"I'll tell! I'll tell!" she shouted.

"Who?" I said for the last time.

"You forgot . . ." She started to giggle. "You forgot to invite Josh Greene!"

"Josh Greene!" I shouted back as I turned on the shower full blast.

She screeched. "That's not fair. I told you."

66

"Josh Greene at my party? What an insult!"

"You better get wet too," she gurgled.

So I did.

Sunday I hung out with my dad all day.

First, I watched him play softball with his buddies. Boring.

Next, we ate pizza. Delicious.

Then we went to an old sci-fi horror film, *The Blob*. A little blob on a man's hand eats him up, which of course makes it a bigger blob. Then the blob gets bigger and bigger as it rolls through the city devouring all the people in its path. Scary.

When we pulled up in front of the house Dad kissed me good-bye and said, "I'll take you to dinner Friday night. Okay?"

"Sure," I answered. Then I asked him, "Dad, do you miss Mop?"

He heaved a big sigh. "I sure do, but mostly I miss you."

"Yeah," I said, "I miss you too."

Before I went to bed I put stamps on my invitations and put the pile next to my book bag so I'd be sure to mail them on the way to school the next morning. Then I reached under my pillow, where I had hidden a blank invitation.

I sat at my desk and filled it out, adding at the bottom in neat script, "Please come to my party. Love, Aviva." I put it in the envelope and addressed it to my dad.

"I'm going to be a chorus girl. You know, tap dancing and all that," Rita announced.

Everyone had gotten my invitations, so during lunch we were talking about what costumes to wear.

"Ah come on, you can't dance. You never took a dancing lesson in your life," I teased her.

"Well, it's not like I have to dance or anything. I'm just going to *look* like a chorus girl." Rita grinned at us as she continued to munch on her diet lunch of carrot sticks and cottage cheese.

"Hah!" Louise sneered. "You're just showing off because you're bigger than the rest of us." She sounded nasty. "You want an excuse for wearing fishnet stockings, spike heels, and shorts," she continued.

"Fishnet stockings? Terrific. I hadn't thought of that," Rita answered her. "I bet you're going as a witch, Louise."

"I'm going as a princess," Janet interrupted.

"Again?" we asked in unison. Janet was *always* a princess—every year since first grade and my first annual Halloween/birthday party.

Rita, Louise, and Janet only dress in costumes that they think make them look pretty. It's one of the basic rules of the glamour-girl clique. And the safest pretty thing to be is a princess, with pastel makeup, a gown, and glitter in your hair.

Since I don't belong to the clique I get to be anything I want, which is always an animal.

"Which animal are you going to be this year?" Sue asked.

"It's a surprise," I told her. Actually I didn't have any ideas for my costume yet.

"You were a rabbit in first grade," Rita said.

"Then a cat. That was my favorite," Louise added.

"A lion in the third grade," I remembered.

"And a parrot last year," added Sue.

"We're missing one," I said.

"A mouse. You were a mouse in fourth grade when I was Princess Leia from *Star Wars*," beamed Janet.

Sue kicked me under the table and groaned, "Aviva, behind you."

I looked up. Josh and Cioffi were beside my chair. Josh had his hands behind his back.

"Why not be a turkey, turkey? That way you won't need a costume," Josh suggested.

"Yeah, Aviva," snarled Cioffi. "Thanks for the invitation. We'll be there."

Josh brought his hand out from behind his back. He was shaking a soda can. Before I could duck out of the way, he let it fizz all over my face.

"You airbrain," I screamed. "You know you're not invited to my party. So bug off. And don't you dare show up!" I added.

"Watch out for the ghosts, turkey," Josh warned with a little evil laugh over his shoulder as he walked away.

After school on Friday I looked over my collage things while I watched TV. It was due the Monday after my party, and I hadn't thought about it in weeks.

Mop nuzzled curiously in my DAD box. I gently pushed him away and lined up the stuff from the box in front of me: a pizza box label, a cigarette, half of my baby undershirt, a picture of Dad with half of me and half of Mop. I picked up the photograph and looked at my dad. His hand rested on my shoulder, and he was grinning proudly at the top of my head instead of into the camera. What a great smile! I missed my dad. Well, Mop wouldn't be seeing much of Dad anymore. I cut the half of Mop from the picture. Then I Scotch-taped it to the other half of him in the photo in my MOM box. Now that I was living with Mom almost all the time, should I cut the half of me from Dad's side of the picture and paste it to the Mom side too?

I started to cut myself away from my Dad, but I just couldn't do it. Poor Dad. All alone looking at the ground. No Aviva. No Mop. I just couldn't do that to him.

I imagined him in that little apartment. All alone night after night. Or was that blond lady staying there all the time now that I wasn't there at all? Were her dumb kids sleeping in my room? What did she do with her old TV then, throw it out the window?

Maybe going back and forth between the two houses wasn't so terrible. Hardly ever seeing my Dad certainly was awful.

I put my collage boxes away and thought and thought and thought. I hardly paid any attention to "The Brady Bunch."

"Mom," I said when she came home from work, "can I stay at Dad's next week, just like the calendar says? Maybe he can help me figure out a costume. He always has good ideas for things like that."

Mom gave me a little smile. "Your dad would like that. You sure it's what you want to do, though? What about Mop?"

I looked at my sweet old dog, spread out like a rug in front of the TV set. Sound asleep.

"He'll be all right here," I told her. "Why don't I just go pack my suitcase."

And I did.

CHAPTER EIGHT

OCTOBER

Dad 17	Dad 18	Dad 19	Dad 20	Dad 21	Dad / Mom 22	Mom 23

MOP LUMBERED SLEEPILY INTO MY BEDROOM WHILE I WAS packing. When he saw the suitcase he gave out a happy "yap-yap," licked my leg, and started nuzzling through my suitcase in search of the dog biscuits I always pack for him.

Dear old Mop. I wish I could explain to you why I just have to live with Dad half of the time and why you can't come with me. I'll miss you.

I went to the kitchen to get some biscuits to distract him while I finished packing. The phone rang. It was Sue. "Aviva," she began without even saying hello, "let's start working on our costumes really early tomorrow. Okay? I already got a whole pile of newspapers to use for the papier-mâché, and . . ." She rattled on and on.

I'd forgotten that Sue was coming to Mom's Saturday afternoon and sleeping over so we could make our Halloween costumes together. We didn't know what we were going to be yet, only that we'd use papier-mâché and make our best costumes *ever!*

"So what do you think, Aviva? What time do you want me to come over?"

"Ah, gee, I'm not sure," I answered as I listened to my dad's car pull up in the driveway.

What am I going to do? Dad's picking me up *now* to stay at his place for a week, and Sue is coming to my mom's in the morning.

"Ah . . ." I stalled. "I'll know in an hour, though. Call you then."

"You sound funny. Is everything all right?" Sue asked.

"Yeah. Fine. Everything's fine." The doorbell rang. "Someone's at the door, Sue. Company. Gotta go. Call you later."

"Listen, Aviva. I have a great idea for the animal you should be this year. But I'm not going to tell you until tomorrow. Want to guess?"

"Later. Gotta go." And I hung up.

"This spaghetti isn't half-bad, Dad. And the place looks really nice."

Dad smiled at me over his second helping. "Thanks. Want some more?"

"Nah. I had plenty already." I smiled back.

Actually Dad's spaghetti was pretty sticky, but the apartment did look good, and my bedroom was sort of cheery with the little yellow curtain and plaid bedspread.

"Dad," I asked. "Do you think Sue could come over here tomorrow, maybe sleep over?"

All during the trip to Dad's and during supper I had wondered what to do about Sue. There was no way around it. I couldn't get out of my date with Sue without lying. And I was sick and tired of lying to my very best friend.

Dad said that it was about time Sue saw our new place, and besides, he had a date Saturday night. "Perfect," he said, "you'll have company." So I called and told her we'd pick her up at eleven the next morning. What I didn't tell her on the phone was that my parents were divorcing and we'd be staying at my dad's new apartment.

The next morning Sue and I climbed the back stairs

to the apartment while Dad went up on the elevator with her overnight bag and two big shopping bags full of supplies for our costumes.

I wondered why I hadn't told Sue about the separation before. It was easy enough to explain. "Trial separations are pretty common now," I told her between the fourth and fifth floors. "Lots of couples do it. Then after a while they get back together. I've seen it happen lots on the soap operas."

"Yeah." Sue stopped to catch her breath at the landing. "I know what you mean." And that's all she said about it. She was much more interested in our costumes. "Come on, Aviva, guess what my idea is for your animal." We had started the sixth flight of stairs.

By the ninth floor Sue finally told me. "A giraffe. That's what you should be this year, a giraffe. I even figured out a way to build a neck for you. It'll take a long time, but it will be the best, the very best costume ever."

All afternoon we worked on it while Dad corrected his college students' papers. Then around seven o'clock he went out for the whole evening and we had the place to ourselves. We made our own supper: elbow macaroni with butter, salt, and pepper; carrot sticks; and ice cream. We pretended we were all finished with school, had jobs, and shared an apartment—like Laverne and Shirley.

"This is a terrific way to live," Sue observed. "No pesty brothers to bother you."

Yeah, I thought, and no divorcing parents. Dad's apartment would be just perfect for two girls out on their own.

This is how we made the giraffe neck. Sue had some really long balloons, which I blew up to be four feet long. I practically fainted doing that. Sue made a paste by mixing flour with water in my dad's new spaghetti pot. Then we dipped strips of newspaper in the paste and wrapped them around the balloon, layer after layer. We did the same thing with an oval-shaped balloon for the head. The problem was that the balloons kept breaking when we here halfway through. Then we had a gloppy, sticky mess and had to start all over.

This is how many balloons it took before we got it right. Three for the neck and five for the head.

"How am I going to breathe and see?" I asked Sue as I studied the four-foot-long papier-mâché neck that would fit over my head.

"Easy. We'll cut holes in some of the brown spots on the neck." Sue had it all figured out.

"Yeah, I guess that'll work," I agreed.

By ten o'clock we were putting the ears and horns on my giraffe's head, but we still hadn't come up with a good enough idea for Sue's costume.

I looked over the kitchen area. What a mess! Flour dust everywhere, globs of goo from the half-wrapped broken balloons stuck to the floor and counter. I picked up two of them and put one on each hand.

"Sue Crandall," I said in my most menacing voice as I took slow heavy steps in her direction, "you are about to be devoured by the Blob."

"Oh . . . oh . . ." she screamed as she backed away.

I stopped in my monster tracks. A thousand light bulbs switched on in my head. "I got it! I know what you can be for Halloween." Why hadn't I thought of it before? "The Blob. It's perfect."

"That disgusting ugly thing in the horror movie that eats everybody up and gets so humungous?" she asked with a disgusted wrinkled-face look.

"Isn't it great? Everybody's seen the movie, right? Besides, it would be fun to make, and easy. Sue the Blob."

She grinned from ear to ear. "Terrific!"

It was fun to make, but not so easy. We covered an old piece of canvas with lumps of pasty newspapers. Then added all the clumpy half-covered balloons that broke when we were working on the giraffe.

We didn't go to bed until one o'clock. As soon as we got in bed, my dad came in. I heard the door close and the light switch go on. He groaned when he saw the living room filled with papier-mâché balloons.

Early the next morning our papier-mâché was dry enough to paint. Yellow with brown spots for the giraffe. Dark green with drips of blood for the Blob.

We were almost finished painting when Dad finally got up.

It was hard for him to appreciate our best costumes ever with his kitchen and living room in such a big mess. But after we'd finished cleaning and were marching around the living room to practice seeing and breathing in our papier-mâché cocoons he had to admit, "The best. The very best costumes ever. Now I'm taking you two out to brunch to celebrate."

"Let's wear them to the car," I suggested to Sue.

"Yeah!" she agreed.

I headed for the door. CRASH. I knocked my head off. CLUMP. Sue bumped into the doorjamb. I was too tall to fit through the door, and Sue was too wide.

After we got my head stuck back onto my neck I carried it out the door. Sue lifted her costume partway off and tipped it to the right in order to get through. This was very difficult since we got a serious case of the Blob giggles.

"You know," Sue told me when we went to the ladies' room at the restaurant, "you're lucky to get to be alone with your mother and father. Living at my house is like living at Grand Central Station. I never get to be alone with anybody."

Later I studied her over my french toast. I couldn't believe that Sue wasn't just crazily happy about being a family. Wasn't it just the best thing ever to have brothers and sisters? Didn't she appreciate being as good as a TV family?

"Thanks for everything, Mr. Granger," Sue said later when we stopped in front of her house. Dad opened the trunk so she could get her costume out. "Put it on," I suggested, "and ring your doorbell."

Dad and I stood by the car and watched. It was perfect. Her little brother—superpest—answered the door. He gave out a long, high-pitched scream and slammed the door. Finding the bloody Blob at your front door on Halloween night is one thing. At two o'clock on a Sunday afternoon is a different matter.

As we drove away, "Sue the Blob" was making her way around the back of the house. We could see her father and brother playing basketball, totally unaware of the terror creeping toward them through the hedges.

"I got your party invitation, honey," Dad told me the next morning at breakfast.

"Are you coming?" I asked him.

Please say yes, I prayed.

"I'll come," he agreed, "for a little while. After all, it is your birthday."

Yeah, I thought, my birthday. My mom and dad are extra sentimental about my birthday. They're always saying things like, "You were born on Halloween because you're such a treat."

I thought it through on the bus to school. They've been getting along much better since I ran away. No fighting when they told me I would stay at Mom's more. And when Dad picked me up he came in to see Mop for a few minutes. Maybe he just wanted to see Mom. My birthday is definitely the perfect time to get my parents back together. Maybe my present from my parents this year will be to say that the divorce is over.

On the way to my seat I left this note on Sue's desk:

Dear Blob,
    Don't tell anyone about my costume especially don't let J.G. know what I'll be on Halloween.

              Your Friend

P.S. Don't tell ANYONE about my mom and dad either.

P.P.S. TEAR This note up.

While Sister was taking attendance Sue turned around and gave me an "okay" sign.

This is what happened during the rest of my DAD week. We learned how to make Shake 'N' Bake chicken, Dad burned rice, and we had his sticky spaghetti two nights in a row.

CHAPTER NINE

Mom	Mom	Mom	Mom	Mom	Mom
24	25	26	27	28	29

MOP WAS BARKING EXCITEDLY ON THE OTHER SIDE OF THE door when I got to Mom's after school on Friday. As soon as I came in he started jumping all over me and licking my face until he knocked me on the couch. Then he jumped on my lap like he was a puppy. Has a 150-pound dog ever jumped on your lap and licked your face?

When he did it again after dinner, Mom said, "Mop really missed you. I don't think it's such a good idea for him to be alone for so long every day."

"Why don't I come visit him after school, even when I'm at Dad's?" I suggested.

"No, that won't work. It's too much traveling for you. You'd get back to Dad's too late," she explained.

I looked into Mop's sparkly blue eyes and threw my leftover hamburger in the direction of his food bowl so he'd get off my lap.

"I think we should hire somebody to dog-sit after school the weeks that you're at your dad's," Mom said.

"Hmm." I thought about that. "Another kid, huh?" I thought some more. "It'd have to be someone who really loves animals. I'd have to interview them to be sure they were qualified."

"Of course," Mom agreed. "Why don't you put up a sign on the community bulletin board at Jason's Su-permarket?"

So I did. This is what the sign said:

```
        Dog-Sitting Job
  after school every other week
        Elm Street Area
       Must love animals!
  Call after 3:30 and evenings
```

I wrote out our phone number fifteen times sideways at the bottom and made little cuts between them so people could just tear off the slips and not have to copy the number down or try to remember it.

Tuesday afternoon I got the first call answering my ad. It was an eighth-grader. "Why do you want this job?" I asked her over the phone.

"Because I need the money to buy makeup and new clothes," she answered.

"Sorry," I told her. "The job's already taken." And I hung up.

The next call was from a high school kid. Thomas Manzo was his name. He didn't want to discuss the job over the phone, so I told him to come over for an interview.

When I opened the door he shifted his briefcase from one hand to another and unbuttoned his sports jacket before shaking my hand. He was very business-like.

Before he sat down he asked, "Where's the lady or gentleman of the house?"

"It's my dog," I said. He looked me over, sat down, and resigned himself to talking to a kid.

Thomas Manzo took out his wallet, opened it, and pulled out a business card, which he handed to me. "My card," he explained.

```
MANZO'S DOG WALKING SERVICE
          Dependable.
References available upon request.

              725-0693
```

"How many dogs do you walk?" I asked him as I studied the card.

"At the same time, or how many clients do we service in all?" he asked me back.

"Both," I said. This was the kind of guy who could definitely get on your nerves.

"We service over a hundred clients in town. I have twenty trained walkers. Our average number of dogs on a walk is five," he answered in his crisp businessman's voice. He eyed Mop, who was spread out on the rug in front of the TV. "With that big guy, there'd probably only be two other dogs. But then, of course, your rate would be higher."

"Do you like dogs?" I asked.

"Listen, it's my business," he answered.

I glared at him.

"Well, of course I like dogs," he added cautiously. "I wouldn't be in the business if I didn't, now would I?"

He called to Mop. "Don't I like dogs, big fella? Come here, Mop. Come see me." Mop got up and walked out of the room without even looking at him.

"I'll think about it," I told Thomas Manzo of Manzo's Dog Walking Service as I showed him to the door. Cripes!

On Wednesday I interviewed Mary Scanlon. She

liked dogs, all right, and Mop liked her. But she could only do the job on Tuesdays. On Mondays she took tennis lessons, on Wednesdays dancing lessons, on Thursdays flute, and on Fridays she had Girl Scouts.

Ian Kelley thought it would be a great job for him, but he was only five years old.

Sue said she'd love to walk Mop for me but that she'd be too busy with the new baby. "You better believe I'd rather pick up after Mop than change dirty diapers," she added.

Rita would have done it, but she's afraid of big dogs. Janet said she wouldn't be caught dead picking up after a dog. "Couldn't I just let him do it when no one's looking and just leave it there?" she asked. "After all, it's biodegradable."

Some people!

Thursday my Mom pulled a not very nice surprise on me. "We're having company for dinner," she announced when I called to tell her I was home from school. Ordinarily I love having company for dinner. Mostly because it means we have cheesecake from Gosman's Bakery for dessert.

"Who's coming?" I asked her.

"My friend George O'Connell. He's been wanting to meet you. And tonight's his birthday. We'll put candles on the Gosman's cheesecake. I'll pick it up on my way home."

"Oh," was all I could say.

When Mom got home she took a shower, put on her prettiest blue dress, and set the table with our best dishes and candles. She wanted me to put on a dress too, but I just changed into a clean T-shirt.

"I've heard so many nice things about you from

84

your mother," was the first thing George said to me. Then he shook my hand like Thomas Manzo did.

"Yeah," I said. "Nice to meet you."

But it wasn't nice at all. It was boring. This is what I said during supper. Nothing. Well, practically nothing. George asked me lots of questions like: "How's school going?" And, "Weren't you scared in the woods all by yourself?" And, "Do you like to play ping-pong?"

These are the only answers George "What's-his-name" got out of me: "Fine." "No." And, "Yes."

When I went to the kitchen to get a biscuit for Mop and a glass of milk for me, I heard Mom say to George, "Don't rush her. She'll like you soon enough."

Fat chance, I thought as I looked at them through a crack in the kitchen door. George was fatter than my dad. He had greasy black hair—not nice and fluffy like my Dad's. And he was a first-class boring person. Mop was giving George the same treatment he gave Thomas Manzo of Manzo's Dog Walking Service, so I knew he agreed with me.

Just then George leaned over and gave my mom a big kiss *right on the mouth*, and my mom let him do it.

I didn't stay up for the cheesecake.

English class on Friday afternoons is for silent reading from "great literature." It's reading whatever you want as long as it's from the classics section of the school library.

I was reading *Alice in Wonderland* by Lewis Carroll. I was up to the chapter on the Mad Hatter's tea party. Alice was pretty annoyed with the silliness and rudeness of the Mad Hatter and the March Hare.

"She got up in great disgust, and walked off: the Dormouse fell asleep instantly, and neither of the others took the least notice of her going, though she looked back once or twice, half hoping that they would call after her: the last time she saw them, they were trying to put the Dormouse into the teapot.

" 'At any rate I'll never go *there* again!' said Alice, as she picked her way through the wood. 'It's the stupidest tea-party I ever was at in all my life!' "

Well, I thought, my party isn't going to be anything like *that* party. I could just picture it. *Halloween night. The room is decorated with orange and black crepe paper and balloons. There are bowls of candy and popcorn all around and Mop has a big orange ribbon around his neck. Everyone is having a terrific time. The costumes are especially good this year. I don't have my giraffe neck on because we're sitting on the floor eating pizza and drinking apple cider. We're planning where to start our trick-or-treating. I look up at my mom, leaning against the kitchen doorway watching us. She has on her pretty blue dress and a yellow rose in her hair. A dozen roses came that afternoon. No name on the card, just "love always" in a familiar handwriting.*

The doorbell rings. Mom and I go to the hall to answer it. It's my dad. First he gives me a kiss, then he gives my mom a big kiss. "Shall we give Aviva her present now?" he asks my mom.

Mom smiles at Dad. "Why not?"

"What is it?" I ask, even though I know.

"Aviva," my dad says, "your mother and I are getting back together. We'll be a family again."

We hug and kiss one another. Then we join my friends in the living room. When Sue sees my parents arm in arm, she gives me a questioning look. I give her an "okay" sign, so she's the only one there who knows what a wonderful birthday present I've gotten.

"Ten more minutes left in this period." Sister's voice interrupted my daydream. I turned the page in *Alice in Wonderland* to the next chapter. A card fell out of the back of the book. It was one of my party invitations, with drops of red Magic Marker blood all over the witch's costume. I opened the card. It was mine, all right, only what I wrote on the inside was crossed out. And this is what it said:

WHAT? ~~a Party~~ GET AVIVA!

WHEN? October 30Th ~~at 6:00 P.M.~~
       WHEN SHE LEAST EXPECTS IT!
WHERE? 110 Elm Street

WHO—OO—OO? aviva Granger

WHY? BECAUSE SHE'S A TURKEY!

Josh pretended he was reading, but he was really smirking and watching me out of the corner of his eye.

"You don't scare me," I hissed as I threw the invitation back at him.

When we got out of school, Josh waved the invitation and yelled, "Hey, Cioffi, guess what? Aviva gave me an invitation to her party. Wanna come?" Then he hollered at me, "Thanks for the invitation, Aviva. See ya tomorrow." And he gave his most evil laugh.

The creep.

CHAPTER TEN

I LOVED THE BEGINNING OF MY HALLOWEEN PARTY. SUE came early so we could put on our costumes and answer the door together.

Janet, Rita, and Louise arrived right after Sue. Janet was in her prettiest princess costume ever—a gown of pink crinoline and satin. She tottered right over to the hall mirror on her very high heels. "It's my mom's senior prom gown," she told us as she checked out her makeup and added some more lipstick to her already pink lips.

Rita was right behind her. "A giraffe!" she exclaimed when she saw me. "It looks so real." Louise pointed to Sue. "Egads! What's that?"

"Guess," Sue said in her canvas-filtered monster voice.

Janet beamed her prettiest princess smile as she patted Sue's costume. "She's sort of cute, don't you think? Like a cookie monster who got caught in a blender."

"Looks like a mound of mud to me," Louise commented.

"Ah! Gross!" Janet exclaimed as she jumped away from "Sue the Blob."

"Think movies," I hinted.

"I know," Rita said, "that pile of stuff in *Close En-*

counters that everyone kept making out of mashed potatoes and dirt and stuff. Right? Great idea," she added.

I was beginning to feel guilty. The Blob costume was *my* idea. I took off my giraffe neck so I could speak more clearly. "Wrong," I told Rita. "Think horror movies."

Sue trudged toward Janet, ready for the kill. "I eat everyone in sight, so I get bigger and bigger and bigger."

"Ick!" Janet exclaimed as she daintily backed off.

"I got it!" Rita yelled. "The Blob. Like in that old movie. How clever."

"See," I said to Sue with relief. "I told you everyone would recognize what you are."

Rita leaned against the front door, put three sticks of gum in her mouth and chewed loudly. "So, what do you think Louise and I are?"

I checked them over. Black fishnet stockings, shorts, spike heels, bright makeup. "It's pretty obvious. You're chorus girls, just like you said you'd be."

"Nope," Rita said as she took off her spike heels.

"So what *are* you?" Sue asked.

"We're both waitresses," Louise giggled, "who *used to be* chorus girls." Right then a group of five more kids arrived. So we started the "guess-what-I-am" business all over again.

This is how many kids guessed what Sue was. None. So we made a sign and pinned it to one of her bumps—"The Blob."

Around seven everyone had arrived. So had four pizzas from Mario's Pizza Parlor. We all sat around on the living room floor eating pizza and drinking apple cider.

"What do you think Cioffi and Greene will do to crash the party?" Janet asked.

"I think they'll try to sneak in wearing costumes," Rita suggested.

"They wouldn't dare try to come in," I said. "I think the trouble will start when we're all out trick-or-treating. Don't forget, nobody call me by my name. I don't want Josh to know who I am." I glanced gratefully at my giraffe head leaning against the fireplace next to a pile of birthday presents.

By seven-thirty everything at my party was exactly like my daydream about it. Black and orange crepe paper and balloons, dishes of candy and popcorn, everyone sitting on the living room floor eating pizza. Mop—with a big orange ribbon around his neck—sniffing all around. My mom even had on her pretty blue dress and was smiling at the whole scene from the kitchen doorway. I smiled back at her. Now, I thought. Now's when my dad should ring the doorbell.

And it rang.

I jumped up. "I'll get it." Dad's timing couldn't have been better, I thought, as I ran to the front door.

I opened it. But no one was there. "Dad?" I called into the evening. SPLAT. Something hit me on the forehead. Goo dribbled down my face. Yucky egg white slithered into my mouth. That's when I screamed. Everyone came running into the hall to see what happened. I slammed the door shut just in time. SPLAT. SPLAT. Two more eggs hit the door.

"Good thing you didn't have on your costume," Sue consoled me as she helped me clean the raw egg off my face in the kitchen.

"It's Greene and Cioffi all right," Janet yelled from her post at the front window. "If I get egg on this dress, my mother will kill me!"

"Josh Greene is asking for trouble from me," I told Sue as we went back into the living room.

Just as I sat down the doorbell rang again.

No one moved.

"Just ignore it," my mom suggested.

What if it's my dad? I thought. "I'm not afraid," I told everyone as I took my yellow slicker off the rack in the front hall and put it on. Then I grabbed the bucket of sand that we keep next to the door to throw on icy steps in the winter.

"Who is it?" I said through the door.

"It's George. Hey, did you know there's raw egg all over your door?"

I just stood there.

"Who is it?" Mom called from the kitchen.

I didn't answer her and hesitated a few seconds before opening the door. That would give Josh time to wind up and land a raw egg on George's dopey head. No splats, so I opened the door.

"Happy birthday, Aviva," he said as I closed the door behind him. He looked at my yellow slicker and the bucket of sand. "I know, don't tell me. You're a fireman—woops, a fire*woman*. Or is it a fire*person*?" he asked my mom, who had met us in the hallway.

"I'm a giraffe," I said without even looking at him as I turned to go back to my friends and my party. George and Mom followed me.

"Who's that?" Rita asked. "Your uncle or something?"

I didn't answer her.

"Here, Aviva." George handed me a little box

wrapped in rainbow wrapping paper. "Here's a little birthday present from me. Why don't you open it now."

"I open my presents later," I said. My mom was glaring at me.

"Thanks," I added as I threw his package on the pile of presents.

"Open your presents now," Louise suggested, "so we can go trick-or-treating."

"Yeah," everyone screamed. "Open your presents. Open them."

"Yes," my mom added as George put his arm around her, "I think it's time."

I got blue eye shadow and mascara from Janet, which is pretty silly since I don't wear makeup yet.

Sue gave me a beautiful book on the animals of Africa with loads of color photographs.

The doorbell rang again. This time it was a long steady high-pitched ring that wouldn't stop.

"Uh-oh—more tricks," someone said.

"I'll take care of it," announced George in an "I'm-the-only-man-here-so-I'll-take-charge" voice.

I followed him into the hall. He opened the door. No one was there. He went outside and came back in a second holding a straight pin between his thumb and index finger. He closed the door. "Just as I thought," he explained as he studied the pin, "the old pin-in-the-doorbell trick."

Just then, while George was showing me the pin, my dad walked in the front door. George turned to see who it was.

"Hi," Dad said, "I'm Aviva's dad. How's the party going?"

"Dad!" I exclaimed. He gave me a big happy-birthday kiss, then shook hands with George.

"Who's father are you?" Dad asked him.

"Ah . . ." George stumbled, "nobody's. I mean nobody's here. I'm George O'Connell."

George turned to my mother, who had just come into the hall to see what was going on. "I'm Jan's friend," he finished.

Mom seemed annoyed at Dad. "You didn't tell me you were coming by, Roy."

I grabbed my dad's hand. I didn't tell her he was coming because I wanted it to be a surprise. Some surprise.

Louise yelled from the living room, "Hurry up, Aviva. We want to go trick-or-treating."

I pulled on my dad's arm. "Dad, come on and see everyone's costumes. You'll never guess what Rita and Louise are this year."

Dad didn't even look at me. He was too busy glaring at Mom and George. "I'm leaving. We'll celebrate your brithday when you come *home* tomorrow."

"No," dumb George finally said. "I'll go." He looked at his watch. "I've got some errands to run anyway." He glanced at my mom. "I'll call you later, Jan." He opened the door. "Nice meeting you," he mumbled to my dad. And "Happy birthday, Aviva," he added as he closed the door.

After George left, the three of us stood in the hall not saying anything. My parents glared at each other with cold, mean stares. It certainly wasn't turning out like my daydream.

"Well, Jan," my father finally broke the silence. "That was really considerate of you."

"Come see everyone's costumes, Dad," I tried again.

"I'm talking to your mother," Dad said sternly. "Go open your presents."

"I have nothing to say to you, Roy," my mom said as she stomped toward the kitchen.

Dad followed her and I went back to the party.

"Hurry, Aviva," Rita complained. "Finish opening your presents so we can go outside."

I rattled the paper as loud as I could to cover the fight going on in the kitchen.

And I said real loud, "Oh, this is terrific." And, "What a great gift." And, "Oh, boy, just what I wanted," to try to cover up my parents' arguing.

But everybody could hear my mom saying, "Tough, Roy, just tough. You don't hide that blond chick of yours under a bushel basket, now do you?" And my dad answering, "At least I'm not parading her in front of Aviva's friends and including her in a kid's birthday party." And, "Look, Roy, all I know is Aviva was staying with you when she ran away. I'm not about to forget *that*."

"You forgot to open this one." Janet pushed George's little rainbow-covered box into my hand.

I threw it back at her and screamed toward the kitchen as loud as I could, "Stop it. Stop it *now!*"

I ran into my bedroom, locked the door, and hid in my closet to cry . . . and cry . . . and cry.

Mom knocked on my door, but I didn't budge.

Dad knocked on my door and called, "I'm sorry, Aviva. Please open the door." But I didn't.

After a while I could hear my dad leave, then all the kids leaving to go trick-or-treating. That's when I got out of the stuffy closet and lay on the bed.

Well, that's pretty much it, I thought. My mom and dad aren't going to get back together. It was just like the old days—yelling and screaming whether anyone was around or not. "Your father and I make each other miserable," was the way Mom had explained it to me when I got back from camp. They make me pretty miserable too, I finally admitted to myself, when they fight like that. Well, good-bye, family.

Mop scratched on the door to be let in. When I opened it, he jumped up and knocked me on the bed. I struggled to get past his wet kisses. "It's all right, Mop," I assured him. "Everything's going to be okay."

Sue came in right behind Mop. She'd been crying. I sat up. "Sue, what's wrong?" I asked.

She plopped beside me and Mop on the bed, her shoulders slumped as she studied her blue sneakers with the rainbow shoelaces I'd given her. "I just feel so sad for you, Aviva, going through all that trouble to make a great costume and not even going trick-or-treating."

I thought about Sue's great costume. She should have gone with the others. "You can still go," I said. "Besides, I can wear my costume next year."

"But we'll be in junior high school next year. We'll probably go to a dance or something."

"I'll always go trick-or-treating," I assured her.

"Well, how about right now?" Sue pleaded.

My mom came to the doorway of my room. She had been crying too. "Listen, girls, I'm going to walk Mop. Why don't you two catch up with the others?"

"That's what I just said, Mrs. Granger," Sue told her.

I looked at my mom. Before I was sad. Now I was really mad. She and Dad had ruined my party. Mom didn't let my stare keep her away, though. She came in and put her arm around me.

I pulled away. Tears were coming to my eyes again, and I didn't want to cry in front of Sue.

"I'll get my costume," Sue said as she jumped off the bed. "And Mop's leash." Mop yapped happily and followed her out of the room.

Mom didn't try to put her arm around me again. She put her hands in her lap and said quietly, "I'm sorry. Dad and I just don't get along. I'm so sorry, baby." And that's all she said.

"I know," I told her. I left her sitting there and ran after Sue.

"Sue," I said. "I'll go trick-or-treating, only we've got to have a plan so I can really get Josh." I went to the refrigerator and carefully placed eight raw eggs in my jacket pockets.

"Oh, Aviva," Sue warned. "Be careful."

"I know what I'm doing," I assured her. "Now listen. You go out the front way with Mom and Mop. I'm going out the back way to Maple Street. I'll meet you at the corner of Colchester and Elm in about ten minutes."

"Okay," Sue agreed as she covered herself with her Blob canvas. "But be careful, Aviva. Remember, he's real tough. In the fourth grade he broke Leonard Thomson's nose in two places."

I listened to the front door close and lock before I went out the back. I put on my neck and head, ducked through the doorway, took a deep breath, and whispered into the dark night, "Watch out, Josh Greene."

I hunched through our yard and around the Smiths' above-ground circular pool. My head pounded; my palms were sweaty.

97

On Maple Street I stood tall and turned my big neck both ways to see who else was on the block. A group of real little kids with their mothers were on a porch about four houses away. No danger there. No one else in sight. I patted my ammunition and crossed the street in the direction of Elm and Colchester.

I am a giraffe. I took longer, more graceful strides. *I move through the grasslands, on the lookout for my natural enemy, the Greene Grunge.*

Trouble was, my viewing eyes were in my neck instead of on top of my long periscope-like head. I couldn't look around without turning my whole body to the left or right.

It was dark and stuffy in there, too. I tried to imagine how nifty my costume looked from the outside. Four feet of giraffe neck with a beautiful small-horned head. Big blue eyes and long eyelashes.

SPLAT! The force of an egg-hit almost knocked my neck off. As I turned my whole body around to face across the street I dug into my pockets for one of my eggs—just in time to catch another egg above my peepholes. I could imagine gooey egg dribbling down my giraffe face.

I was furious. I saw someone moving in the bushes in front of the Smiths'. Swing and hurl. My egg hit the side of Mr. Smith's brand-new station wagon.

''Hey, man,'' a voice behind me yelled to my assailant in the bushes across the street. ''Hey, man, you should see this dude's costume. Lay off the eggs and come see this thing.''

I turned. A tall billowing ghost was behind me. Just as I was about to say, ''Who are you?'' the ghost got a tomato—right between the eyeholes.

"Hey!" the ghost yelled in a deep sheet-veiled voice. "Don't mess with me. Not with me."

I took out one of my eggs. "Gimme that," said the ghost. "I'll take care of him."

I handed him that egg and took out another.

A boy scurried out of the bushes, ran under the streetlamp, and headed toward the Smiths' backyard. Cioffi!

"Let's get him," I shouted.

"You bet," said the ghost as we both took off across the street. I threw off my giraffe neck; the ghost threw off his sheet. Our costumes landed side by side on the Smiths' front lawn as our two eggs got Cioffi on the back.

I turned to grin at my partner. It was Josh! He was as surprised to see me as I was to see him. But this was no time for old grudges.

I went around the right of the house, and Josh took the left side. We cornered Cioffi at the back of the Smiths' garage.

"Josh, don't!" Cioffi pleaded as he backed against the garage wall. Cioffi was out of eggs! We got him with five big ones at close range. Then Josh got even closer to top the job off with shaving cream.

"Do you know what Cioffi is for Halloween?" Josh asked me as he threateningly held the can of shaving cream to Cioffi's eggy hair.

"I have no idea," I answered. "A bum?"

"No," Josh laughed as Cioffi tried to wiggle away from him. "He's Humpty Dumpty. Doesn't that crack you up?"

"I'm the one that's cracked up," Cioffi laughed back. "And I'm going to get you, Greene," he added.

Cioffi grabbed the can of shaving cream and chased Josh around the Smiths' swimming pool.

I left them there and went around to the front yard just as the Smiths turned on the backyard lights to see what was going on. I picked up my costume and went off to find Sue and the others.

After all, it was Halloween night, and I hadn't rung one doorbell yet.

CHAPTER ELEVEN

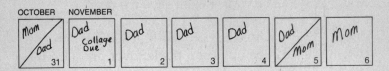

THE FIRST THING I DID WHEN I WOKE UP THE NEXT MORNING was lay out my Halloween loot. I counted out fourteen small candy bars, five packs of gum, four old apples, three popcorn balls, four quarters, three dimes, one nickel, and twenty-nine pennies—and that didn't include all the junk I ate while going from house to house. It was a pretty good haul, considering I got such a late start. I put everything back in my brown treat bag and went into the kitchen.

At breakfast my mom told me, "While you were still sleeping a very nice young man came by to apply for the Mop-walking job. I think we should hire him. You're going back to your father's today, and you've turned down everyone else who's applied."

"Well, no one's been good enough," I explained.

"This boy is," Mom answered. "He loves animals and Mop loved him. I think he's perfect for the job."

"All right," I agreed. My mother was a good judge. She loved Mop almost as much as I did.

Mom rummaged through my treat bag to see if there were any Milky Ways. "Do you want me to call him back and ask him to come over to meet you before you go to your dad's?" she asked.

"I don't have time," I explained. "Dad's picking me up in half an hour and I haven't even packed or anything. If you're sure he'll be good, it's all right with me."

"I'm glad it's settled," Mom said. Then she looked

up from my bag disappointedly. "Did you eat all the Milky Ways? You didn't even save me *one?*"

"Look in the freezer," I told her. She opened the door to find a whole bag of little Milky Ways sitting between the ice cube trays and the leftover pizza from my party.

"Mrs. Smith gave them to me because my costume was so great and because I'm such a good neighbor."

"How nice," Mom said as she juggled the bag from hand to hand. "We'll share them."

What Mrs. Smith said exactly was, "You're such a good girl, not like those rowdy boys who were screaming and running all over our backyard tonight. Why, they even threw eggs at Mr. Smith's new car and all over the garage! I'm so grateful to have a nice girl like you living next door."

"Mom," I said. "You keep all the Milky Ways. I'll be at Dad's." I rattled my treat bag. "Besides, I have lots of candy right here."

As I was throwing my clothes into my suitcase, I stopped to take a slow look around my room. My lion poster would look terrific over my bureau at Dad's. And my mystery book collection would fit just right on the bookshelves. My room at Mom's was absolutely crammed with all my stuff. It would probably look a lot better with less in it.

Mom came in to kiss me good-bye. She smelled all chocolaty from Milky Ways. "After last night I'd rather not be here when Roy picks you up," she said. "I'll go do errands." She gave me a big hug, then stood back to give me a final good look. "Aviva, would you please call me *every* day after school? Even when you're at your Dad's?"

"Sure, Mom," I said.

Mop nuzzled my leg. "Why don't you take Mop with you to the store so he won't have to watch me leave?" I suggested.

"Good idea," she agreed.

But you can't fool good old Mop. He gave me a real sad-eyed look and jumped on me with a big slurpy kiss before he followed my mom out of the room.

After they left I went down to the cellar and got two empty cartons. This is what I packed to put in my bedroom at Dad's:

33 mystery books
4 stuffed animals
1 lion poster
1 *Yellow Submarine* poster
half of my rainbow card collection
half of my seashell collection
1 little braided rug
1 set of Magic Markers
1 set of rainbow bath towels
1 old bathrobe

When Dad and I had loaded all the stuff in the trunk of the car and were sitting in the front seat he turned to me with eyes as sad as Mop's. "I'm sorry about what happened at your party. I promise you it won't happen again."

I gave my dad a tough, serious look. "Cross your heart?" I asked.

"Cross my heart," he said solemnly as he drew a cross over his chest.

When I got to Dad's the first thing I did was put all my stuff away. My room looked nice and cozy. There were colorful books and seashells lined up on the shelves, Magic Markers on my desk, posters on the walls, and rainbow cards on the door. Then, just in case the blond lady came over with her kids when I wasn't there, I made a sign that said Aviva's Place—Keep Out, and Scotch-taped it on the outside of my door.

When my room looked just about perfect, I took out my two boxes of collage things and the big piece of white cardboard Dad had bought for me on the way home.

This is how long it took me to make my collage. Seven and a half hours. I worked on it from twelve noon until eight o'clock at night, with only half an hour out for supper.

The next morning I brought my collage to school covered with brown paper so no one would see it before I gave my talk. I leaned it on the back wall behind my chair. Cioffi and Josh weren't there yet, which was a relief to me. Maybe they were both absent, I thought, most likely playing hooky. As Sister clapped three times to begin the day, Cioffi came through the door.

At ten-thirty sharp Sister announced, "As I told you on Friday, the third row and half of the fourth row will do their reports today." Josh probably was absent because he hadn't done his "Who Am I?" collage. It was one assignment he couldn't copy off me.

"We'll begin at the back of the room. Aviva Granger will go first."

My heart plopped into my stomach with a thud. I got up and slowly carried my collage up the aisle. As I walked to the front of the room, Sister walked to the back and stood behind my chair. When I stood at Sister's desk, Sue gave me a reassuring smile. I pulled the brown paper off my collage and leaned it against the blackboard. I didn't know what to do with my hands, so I picked up Sister's pointer with my right hand and put my other hand behind my back.

I looked up and saw all those eyes staring at me, waiting for me to begin.

Cripes.

"Begin, dear," Sister said.

"I'm Aviva Granger, and this is my 'Who Am I?' collage. I love animals and will be a veterinarian when I grow up." I pointed to the little pictures of animals I had cut out from my old *World* magazines.

"This is my dog, Mop. He lives with me at my mom's house." I pointed to a picture of my mom standing next to me and Mop.

"I love doing outdoor things." I pointed to a picture of a bicycle. "And Chinese food." I pointed to the chopsticks.

"I love to watch TV." I drew the pointer across the collage to show the cut-out letters T and V from magazine and newspaper captions. "Reruns are my favorite shows. I think I'm a little like Lucille Ball in 'I Love Lucy.' I love playing tricks on people in good—"

"Mr. Greene," Sister interrupted my talk. "How nice of you to join us."

Everyone turned toward the door.

"Mornin', Sister," Josh said with a big grin.

"Do you have a late note?" Sister asked.

"No, Sister, I was making my collage." He patted his back dungaree pocket.

"Well, take your place. See me after school about your lateness. You'll present your collage next."

Josh sauntered up Cioffi's row, gave him a quick "we're-the-tough-guys" handclasp, stepped over my seat, and sat down.

105

Sister watched the whole scene in stern silence from her position behind my desk. When Josh finally settled down she looked at me. "Well, *now* you may continue, Aviva."

I looked over my collage to see what I still hadn't explained. There were two photographs cut out like paper dolls. On one side of the collage was my mom, Mop, and me in front of a drawing of our Elm Street house. On the other side was me and Dad in front of a picture of our big apartment building, which I outlined with different kinds of pasta—long spaghetti for the walls, elbow macaroni for the roof tiles.

"There are two pictures of me," I continued, "because my parents are divorced. I live half the time with my mom in our old house"—I pointed to the house—"and half the time with my dad in this big building." I pointed to the pasta apartment building. "It's made out of spaghetti on my collage because that's all Dad and I know how to cook. But we're learning new things."

"One week here," I reviewed, "one week there. Back and forth like that." I pointed to one side, then the other. "Just like"—I pointed to a small white ball in the middle of the collage—"a Ping-Pong ball." I quickly added, "The end."

Sister smiled as she looked around the room. "Does anyone have any questions for Aviva?"

Rita raised her hand. "What's the rainbow for?"

I looked at the big rainbow—the prettiest I had ever made—connecting my two homes. "The rainbow is my symbol," I explained. "I love rainbows. To me they stand for love and peace. That's all."

The class clapped like they always do when people finish a speech. Sister clapped too and smiled at me. "Very good, dear. You've gotten us off to a fine start." I smiled back. What a relief to have that over with. Sister came to the front of the room as I went to the back. She tacked my collage up on the bulletin board, turning around as she was doing it to say, "Next. Josh Greene."

Cioffi guffawed. No one believed Josh had really done the assignment. Not even Sister. So we were all surprised when Josh Greene got up and walked to the front of the room. He stood at Sister's desk and pulled a folded-up piece of paper from his back pocket. He unfolded it and held it across his chest. He looked at it upside down as he spoke in a quiet, shy voice.

Josh Greene was just as embarrassed to speak in front of the class as I had been. "I'm Josh. This is my collage." He pointed to a faded snapshot. "The picture in the corner is my mother and father with me when I was a baby." It was the kind of photo you take in a booth at the penny arcade. A smiling couple holding up a little baby were crammed into the two-inch-square picture. "I don't live with them anymore." Josh explained, "My mother's dead and my father lives in . . ." He paused like he had to make up a place. ". . . in California."

The only other thing on the collage was a large drawing of a big dog. So, I thought, he got a dog after all. I remembered his grandmother scolding him about dogs being too much trouble and too expensive.

Josh pointed to the drawing. "I love animals. I'm going to work in a zoo when I grow up. Animals are very loyal. I like them even more than people. I have a job." He looked at me with a kind of funny little smile. "I take care of this big dog. The pay's good. That's all."

Mop! Josh was the kid my mother hired to walk Mop! Didn't she know that Josh was my archenemy? Didn't he tell her who he was? What nerve. We'd been tricked into hiring Josh Greene—the biggest bully in the school—to take care of my dog. No way was that going to happen, I decided. I can't let it.

Josh was finished. A few kids giggled. One or two clapped. "Thank you, Josh," Sister said. "I'm glad you did the assignment. And that's a very fine drawing you've done," she added. "I think you have real talent."

Sister took Josh's collage and tacked it next to mine.

Josh, I thought as I studied his collage, living alone with his crotchety, sick grandmother. Not even allowed to have a dog. And he really does love animals. His mom dead. His father living who knows where.

Josh sauntered up the aisle to his seat. Some of the kids started laughing. He stopped halfway and announced in a loud voice, "You better watch out when you see me with that dog. He's big and he's mean." The laughing stopped. Sure, I thought, Mop's mean. Just like you are, Josh Greene. And I winked at him. And he winked back.

You can't tell a friend by her looks— or a book by its cover!

MAUDIE AND ME and the DIRTY BOOK

✳ ✳ ✳

By
BETTY MILES

author of *The Trouble With Thirteen*

"To look at me, you'd probably think I was pretty ordinary—except for my feet, which are size 9½M. You wouldn't expect me to get into trouble at school, or wreck little children's minds with dirty books."

For Kate Harris, getting used to life in middle school means figuring out where to sit in the cafeteria, and avoiding kids like Maudie Schmidt. But then Kate and Maudie are thrown together in a school reading project, and a book that Kate reads to some first graders sparks an angry controversy. Kate finds herself in the middle as the whole town takes sides and demands for censorship grow. And in the midst of the uproar, Kate discovers that Maudie is not only her staunchest ally, but a true friend.

AN AVON CAMELOT • 64071-6 • $2.25

"Some kids in our class act as though they can't wait to be teenagers. Some girls even wear green eye shadow to school and pierce their ears. I never want to grow up if that's how you're supposed to act."

The Trouble With Thirteen

by Betty Miles

Annie and her best friend Rachel wish they could stay twelve forever. Everything is perfect ... until unexpected changes begin pulling them apart just when they need each other the most. But through it all, Annie and Rachel learn about independence and loyalty—and some good things about turning thirteen.

An Avon Camelot Book   51136 • $1.95

Also by Betty Miles:

Just The Beginning   59261-4 • $1.95
Looking On   60905-3 • $1.95
The Real Me   63057-5 • $1.95
Maudie And Me and The Dirty Book   64071-6 • $2.25